PENELOPE FITZGERALD was one of the most distinctive voices in English literature. The author of nine novels, three biographies and one collection of short stories, she died in 2000.

From the reviews of *Offshore*:

'This is an astonishing book. Hardly more than 50,000 words, it is written with a manic economy and a tamped-down force that continually explodes in a series of exactly controlled detonations. A marvellous achievement'   *Sunday Times*

'A novel of crisp originality, lucid and expressive with some splendid bursts of satire'   *Observer*

D1386448

By the same author

PENELOPE FITZGERALD

Offshore

FOURTH ESTATE · *London*

Fourth Estate
An imprint of HarperCollins*Publishers*
77–85 Fulham Palace Road, Hammersmith, London W6 8JB

Visit our authors' blog at www.fifthestate.co.uk
Love this book? www.bookarmy.com

This edition is produced exclusively for Waterstone's 2011

First published in Great Britain by Collins in 1979

Previously published in paperback by Flamingo in 1988 and 2003

ISBN 978-0-00-790372-6

Printed and bound in Great Britain by Clays Ltd, St Ives plc

For Grace
and all who sailed in her

'che mena il vento, e che batte la pioggia,
e che s'incontran con sì aspre lingue.'

1

'ARE we to gather that *Dreadnought* is asking us all to do something dishonest?' Richard asked.

Dreadnought nodded, glad to have been understood so easily.

'Just as a means of making a sale. It seems the only way round my problem. If all present wouldn't mind agreeing not to mention my main leak, or rather not to raise the question of my main leak, unless direct enquiries are made.'

'Do you in point of fact want us to say that *Dreadnought* doesn't leak?' asked Richard patiently.

'That would be putting it too strongly.'

All the meetings of the boat-owners, by a movement as natural as the tides themselves, took place on Richard's converted *Ton* class minesweeper. *Lord Jim*, a felt reproof to amateurs, in speckless, always-renewed grey paint, over-shadowed the other craft and was nearly twice their tonnage, just as Richard, in his decent dark blue blazer, dominated the meeting itself. And yet he by no means wanted this responsibility. Living on Battersea Reach, overlooked by some very good houses, and under the surveillance of the Port of London Authority, entailed, surely, a certain standard of conduct. Richard would be one of the last men on earth or water to want to impose it. Yet someone must. Duty is what no-one else will do at the moment. Fortunately he did not have to define duty. War service in the RNVR, and his whole temperament before and since, had done that for him.

Richard did not even want to preside. He would have been happier with a committee, but the owners, of whom several rented rather than owned their boats, were not of the substance from which committees are formed. Between *Lord Jim*, moored almost in the shadow of Battersea Bridge, and the old wooden Thames barges, two hundred yards upriver and close to the rubbish disposal wharfs and the brewery, there was a great gulf fixed. The barge-dwellers, creatures neither of firm land nor water, would have liked to be more respectable than they were. They aspired towards the Chelsea shore, where, in the early 1960s, many thousands lived with sensible occupations and adequate amounts of money. But a certain failure, distressing to themselves, to be like other people, caused them to sink back, with so much else that drifted or was washed up, into the mud moorings of the great tideway.

Biologically they could be said, as most tideline crea-tures are, to be 'successful'. They were not easily dislodged.

But to sell your craft, to leave the Reach, was felt to be a desperate step, like those of the amphibians when, in earlier stages of the world's history, they took ground. Many of these species perished in the attempt.

Richard, looking round his solid, brassbound table, got the impression that everyone was on their best behaviour. There was no way of avoiding this, and since, after all, Willis had requested some kind of discussion of his own case, he scrupulously collected opinions.

'Rochester? Grace? Bluebird? Maurice? Hours of Ease? Dunkirk? Relentless?'

Richard was quite correct, as technically speaking they were all in harbour, in addressing them by the names of their craft. Maurice, an amiable young man, had realised as soon as he came to the Reach that Richard was always going to do this and that he himself would accordingly be known as *Dondeschiepolschuygen IV*, which was inscribed in gilt lettering on his bows. He therefore renamed his boat *Maurice*.

No-one liked to speak first, and Willis, a marine artist some sixty-five years old, the owner of *Dreadnought*, sat with his hands before him on the table and his head slightly sunken, so that only the top, with its spiky crown of black and grey hair, could be seen. The silence was eased by a long wail from a ship's hooter from downstream. It was a signal peculiar to Thames river – I am about to get under way. The tide was making, although the boats still rested on the mud.

Hearing a slight, but significant noise from the galley, Richard courteously excused himself. Perhaps they'd have a little more to contribute on this very awkward point when he came back.

'How are you getting on, Lollie?'

Laura was cutting something up into small pieces, with a cookery book open in front of her. She gave him a weary, large-eyed, shires-bred glance, a glance whose horizons should have been bounded by acres of plough and grazing. Loyalty to him, Richard knew, meant that she had never complained so far to anyone but himself about this business of living, instead of in a nice house, in a boat in the middle of London. She went home once a month to combat any such suggestion, and told her family that there were very amusing people living on the Thames. Between the two of them there was no pretence. Yet Richard, who always put each section of his life, when it was finished with, quietly behind him, and liked to be able to give a rational explanation for everything, could not account for this, his attachment to *Lord Jim*. He could very well afford a house, and indeed *Jim* had been an expensive conversion. And if the river spoke to his dreaming, rather than to his daytime self, he supposed that he had no business to attend to it.

'We're nearly through,' he said.

Laura shook back her dampish longish hair. In theory, her looks depended on the services of many employees, my hairdresser, my last hairdresser, my doctor, my other doctor who I went to when I found the first one wasn't doing me any good, but with or without their attentions, Laura would always be beautiful.

'This galley's really not so bad, is it, with the new extractor?' Richard went on, 'A certain amount of steam still, of course . . .'

'I hate you. Can't you get rid of these people?'

In the saloon Maurice, who had come rather late, was saying something intended to be in favour of Willis. He was incurably sympathetic. His occupation, which was that of picking up men in a neighbouring public house, with which he had a working arrangement, during the evening hours, and bringing them back to the boat, was not particularly profitable. Maurice was not born to make a profit, but then, was not born to resent this, or anything else. Those who felt affection for him had no easy way of telling him so, since he seemed to regard friend and enemy alike. For example, an unpleasant acquaintance of his used part of Maurice's hold as a repository for stolen goods. Richard and Laura were among the few boat owners who did not know this. And yet Maurice appeared to be almost proud, because Harry was not a customer, but somebody who had demanded a favour and given nothing in return.

'I shall have to warn Harry not to talk about the leak either,' he said.

'What does he know about it?' asked Willis.

'He used to be in the Merchant Navy. If people are coming to look at *Dreadnought*, he might be asked his opinion.'

'I've never seen him speak to anyone. He doesn't come often, does he?'

At that moment *Lord Jim* was disturbed, from stem to stern, by an unmistakeable lurch. Nothing fell, because on *Lord Jim* everything was properly secured, but she heaved, seemed to shake herself gently, and rose. The tide had lifted her.

At the same time an uneasy shudder passed through all those sitting round the table. For the next six hours – or a little less, because at Battersea the flood lasts five and a half hours, and the ebb six and a half – they would be living not on land, but on water. And each one of them felt the patches, strains and gaps in their craft as if they were weak places in their own bodies. They dreaded, and were yet painfully anxious, to get back and see whether the last caulking had given way. A Thames barge has no keel and is afloat in the first few inches of shoal water. The only exception was Woodrow, from *Rochester*, the retired director of a small company, who was fanatical in the maintenance of his craft. The flood tide, though it had no real terrors for Woodie, caused him to fret impatiently, because *Rochester*, in his opinion, had beautiful lines below water, and these would not now be visible again for twelve hours.

On every barge on the Reach a very faint ominous tap, no louder than the door of a cupboard shutting, would be followed by louder ones from every strake, timber and weatherboard, a fusillade of thunderous creaking, and even groans that seemed human. The crazy old vessels, riding high in the water without cargo, awaited their owner's return.

Richard, like a good commander, sensed the uneasiness of the meeting, even through the solid teak partition. He would never, if he had taken to the high seas in past centuries, have been caught napping by a mutiny.

'I'd better see them on their way.'

'You can ask one or two of them to stay behind for a drink, if you like,' Laura said, 'if there's anyone possible.'

She often unconsciously imitated her father's voice, and, like him, was beginning to drink a little too much occasionally, out of boredom. Richard felt overwhelmed with affection for her. 'I got *Country Life* to-day,' she said.

He had noticed that already. Anything new was noticeable on shipshape *Lord Jim*. The magazine was lying open at the property advertisements, among which was a photograph of a lawn, and a cedar tree on it with a shadow, and a squarish house in the background to show the purpose of the lawn. A similar photograph, with variations as to size and county, appeared month after month, giving the impression that those who read *Country Life* were above change, or that none was recognised there.

'I didn't mean that one, Richard, I meant a few pages farther on. There's some smaller places there.'

'I might ask Nenna James to stay behind,' Richard said. 'From *Grace*, I mean.'

'Why, do you think she's pretty?'

'I've never thought about it.'

'Hasn't her husband left her?'

'I'm not too sure what the situation is.'

'The postman used to say that there weren't many letters for *Grace*.'

Laura said 'used' because letters were no longer brought by the postman; after he had fallen twice from *Maurice*'s ill-secured gangplank, the whole morning's mail soaked away in the great river's load of rubbish, the GPO, with every reason on its side, had notified the Reach that they could no longer undertake deliveries. They acknowledged that Mr Blake, from *Lord Jim*, had rescued their employee on both occasions and they wished to record their thanks for this. The letters, since this, had had to be collected from the boatyard office, and Laura felt that this made it not much better than living abroad.

'I think Nenna's all right,' Richard continued. 'She

seems quite all right to me, really. I don't know that I'd want to be left alone with her for any length of time.'

'Why not?'

'Well, I'm not quite sure that she mightn't burst into tears, or perhaps suddenly take all her clothes off.' This had actually once happened to Richard at Nestor and Sage, the investment counsellors where he worked. They were thinking of redesigning the whole office on the more modern open plan.

The whole meeting looked up in relief as he came back to the saloon. Firmly planted on the rocking boat, he suggested, even by his stance in the doorway, that things, however difficult, would turn out reasonably well. It was not that he was too sure of himself, simply that he was a good judge of the possible.

Willis was thanking young Maurice for his support.

'Well, you spoke up . . . a friend in need . . .'

'You're welcome.'

Willis half got up from the table. 'All the same, I don't believe that fellow was ever in the Merchant Navy.'

Business suspended, thought Richard. Firmly, but always politely, he escorted the ramshackle assembly up the companion ladder. It was a relief, as always, to be out on deck. The first autumn mists made it difficult to see the whole length of the Reach. Seagulls, afloat like the boats, idled round *Lord Jim*, their white feathers soiled at the waterline.

'You'll probably have plenty of time to do something about your trouble anyway,' he said to Willis, 'it's quite a long business, arranging the sale of these boats. Your leak's somewhere aft, isn't it? . . . you've got all four pumps working, I take it . . . one in each well?'

This picture of *Dreadnought* was so wide of the mark that Willis found it better to say nothing, simply making a gesture which had something in common with a petty officer's salute. Then he followed the others, who had to cross to land and tramp along the Embankment. The middle Reach was occupied by small craft, mostly laying up for the winter, some of them already double lashed down under weather-cloths. These were for fairweather people only. The barge-owners had to go as far as the brewery wharf, across *Maurice*'s foredeck and over a series of gangplanks which connected them with their own boats. Woody had to cross *Maurice, Grace* and *Dreadnought* to rejoin *Rochester*. Only *Maurice* was made fast to the wharf.

One of the last pleasure steamers of the season was passing, with cabin lights ablaze, on its way to Kew. 'Battersea Reach, ladies and gentlemen. On your right, the artistic colony. Folk live on those boats like they do on the Seine, it's the artist's life they're leading there. Yes, there's people living on those boats.'

Richard had detained Nenna James. 'I wish you'd have a drink with us, Laura hoped you would.'

Nenna's character was faulty, but she had the instinct

to see what made other people unhappy, and this instinct had only failed her once, in the case of her own husband. She knew, at this particular moment, that Richard was distressed by the unsatisfactory nature of the meeting. Nothing had been evaluated, or even satisfactorily discussed.

'I wish I knew the exact time,' she said.

Richard was immediately content, as he only was when something could be ascertained to the nearest degree of accuracy. The exact time! Perhaps Nenna would like to have a look at his chronometers. They often didn't work well in small boats – they were affected by changes of temperature – he didn't know whether Nenna had found that – and, of course, by vibration. He was able to give her not only the time, but the state of the tide at every bridge on the river. It wasn't very often that anyone wanted to know this.

Laura put the bottles and glasses and a large plateful of bits and pieces through the galley hatch.

'It smells of something in there.'

There was the perceptible odour of tar which the barge-owners, since so much of their day was spent in running repairs, left behind them everywhere.

'Well, dear, if you don't like the smell, let's go aft,' said Richard, picking up the tray. He never let a woman carry anything. The three of them went into a kind of snug, fitted with built-in lockers and red cushions. A little yacht stove gave out a temperate glow, its draught adjusted to produce exactly the right warmth.

Laura sat down somewhat heavily.

'How does it feel like to live without your husband?' she asked, handing Nenna a large glass of gin. 'I've often wondered.'

'Perhaps you'd like to fetch some more ice,' Richard said. There was plenty.

'He hasn't left me, you know. We just don't happen to be together at the moment.'

'That's for you to say, but what I want to know is, how do you get on without him? Cold nights, of course, don't mind Richard, it's a compliment to him if you think about it.'

Nenna looked from one to the other. It was a relief, really, to talk about it.

'I can't do the things that women can't do,' she said. 'I can't turn over *The Times* so that the pages lie flat, I can't fold up a map in the right creases, I can't draw corks, I can't drive in nails straight, I can't go into a bar and order a drink without wondering what everyone's thinking about it, and I can't strike matches towards myself. I'm well educated and I've got two children and I can manage pretty well, there's a number of much more essential things that I know how to do, but I can't do those ones, and when they come up I feel like weeping myself sick.'

'I'm sure I could show you how to fold up a map,' said Richard, 'it's not at all difficult once you get the hang of it.'

Laura's eyes seemed to have moved closer together. She was concentrating intensely.

'Did he leave you on the boat?'

'I bought *Grace* myself, while he was away, with just about all the money we'd got left, to have somewhere for me and the girls.'

'Do you like boats?'

'I'm quite used to them. I was raised in Halifax. My father had a summer cabin on the Bras d'Or Lake. We had boats there.'

'I hope you're not having any repair problems,' Richard put in.

'We get rain coming in.'

'Ah, the weatherboarding. You might try stretching tarpaulin over the deck.'

Although he tried hard to do so, Richard could never see how anyone could live without things in working order.

'Personally, though, I'm doubtful about the wisdom of making endless repairs to these very old boats. My feeling, for what it's worth, is that they should be regarded as wasting assets. Let them run down just so much every year, remember your low outgoings, and in a few years' time have them towed away for their break-up value.'

'I don't know where we should live then,' said Nenna.

'Oh, I understood you to say that you were going to find a place on shore.'

'Oh, we are, we are.'

'I didn't mean to distress you.'

Laura had had time, while listening without much attention to these remarks, to swallow a further quantity of spirits. This had made her inquisitive, rather than hostile.

'Where'd you get your guernsey?'

Both women wore the regulation thick Navy blue sailing sweaters, with a split half inch at the bottom of each side seam. Nenna had rolled up her sleeves in the warmth of the snug, showing round forearms covered with very fine golden hair.

'I got mine at the cut price place at the end of the Queenstown Road.'

'It's not as thick as mine.'

Laura leaned forward, and, taking a good handful, felt the close knitting between finger and thumb.

'I'm a judge of quality, I can tell it's not as thick. Richard, like to feel it?'

'I'm afraid I can't claim to know much about knitting.'

'Well, make the stove up then. Make it up, you idiot! Nenna's freezing!'

'I'm warm, thank you, just right.'

'You've got to be warmer than that! Richard, she's your guest!'

'I can adjust the stove, if you like,' said Richard, in relief, 'I can do something to the regulator.'

'I don't want it regulated!'

Nenna knew that, if it hadn't been disloyal, Richard would have appealed to her to do or say something.

'We use pretty well anything for fuel up our end,' she began, 'driftwood and washed-up coke and anything that'll burn. Maurice told me that last winter he had to borrow a candle from *Dreadnought* to unfreeze the lock of his woodstore. Then when he was entertaining one of his friends he couldn't get his stove to burn right and he had to keep it alight with matchboxes and cheese straws.'

'It's bad practice to keep your woodstore above deck,' said Richard.

Laura had been following, for some reason, with painful interest. 'Do cheese straws burn?'

'Maurice thinks they do.'

Laura disappeared. Nenna had just time to say, I must be going, before she came back, tottering at a kind of dignified slant, and holding a large tin of cheese straws.

'Fortnum's.'

Avoiding Richard, who got to his feet as soon as he saw something to be carried, she kicked open the top of the Arctic and flung them in golden handfuls onto the glowing bed of fuel.

'Hot!'

The flames leaped up, with an overpowering stink of burning cheese.

'Lovely! Hot! I've got plenty more! The kitchen's full of them! We'll make Richard throw them. We'll all throw them!'

'There's someone coming,' said Nenna.

Footsteps overhead, like the relief for siege victims. She knew the determined stamp of her younger daughter, but there was also a heavier tread. Her heart turned over.

'Ma, I can smell burning.'

After a short fierce struggle, Richard had replaced the Arctic's brass lid. Nenna went to the companion.

'Who's up there with you, Tilda?'

Tilda's six-year-old legs, in wellingtons caked with mud, appeared at the open hatch.

'It's Father Watson.'

Nenna did not answer for a second, and Tilda bellowed:

'Ma, it's the kindly old priest. He came round to *Grace*, so I brought him along here.'

'Father Watson isn't old at all, Tilda. Bring him down here, please. That's to say . . .'

'Of course,' said Richard. 'You'll have a whisky, father, won't you?' He didn't know who he was talking to, but believed, from films he had seen, that RC priests drank whisky and told long stories; that could be useful at the present juncture. Richard spoke with calm authority. Nenna admired him and would have liked to throw her arms round him.

'No, I won't come in now, thank you all the same,' called Father Watson, whose flapping trousers could now be seen beside Tilda's wellingtons against a square patch of sky. 'Just a word or two, Mrs James, I can easily wait if you're engaged with your friends or if it's not otherwise convenient.'

But Nenna, somewhat to the curate's surprise, for he seldom felt himself to be a truly welcome guest, was already half way up the companion. It had begun to drizzle, and his long macintosh was spangled with drops of rain, which caught the reflections of the shore lights and the riding lights of the craft at anchor.

'I'm afraid the little one will get wet.'

'She's waterproof,' said Nenna.

As soon as they reached the Embankment Father Watson began to speak in measured tones. 'It's the children, as you must be aware, that I've come about. A message from the nuns, a message from the Sisters of Misericord.' He sometimes wondered if he would be more successful in the embarrassing errands he was called upon to undertake if he had an Irish accent, or some quaint turn of speech.

'Your girls, Mrs James, Tilda here, and the twelve-year-old.'

'Martha.'

'A very delightful name. Martha busied herself about the household work during our Lord's visits. But not a saint's name, I think.'

Presumably Father Watson said these things automatically. He couldn't have walked all the way down to the Reach from his comfortless presbytery simply to talk about Martha's name.

'She'll be taking another name at confirmation, I assume. That should not long be delayed. I suggest Stella Maris, Star of the Sea, since you've decided to make your dwelling place upon the face of the waters.'

'Father, have you come to complain about the girls' absence from school?'

They had arrived at the wharf, which was exceedingly ill-lit. The brewers to whom it belonged, having ideas, like all brewers in the 1960s, of reviving the supposed jollity of the eighteenth century, had applied for permission to turn it into a fashionable beer garden. The very notion, however, ran counter to the sodden, melancholy, and yet enduring spirit of the Reach. After the plans had been shelved, the whole place had been leased out to various small-time manufacturers and warehousemen; the broken-down sheds and godowns must still be the property of somebody, so too must be the piles of crates whose stencilled lettering had long since faded to pallor.

But, rat-ridden and neglected, it was a wharf still. The river's edge, where Virgil's ghosts held out their arms in longing for the farther shore, and Dante, as a living man, was refused passage by the ferryman, the few planks that mark the meeting point of land and water, there, surely, is a place to stop and reflect, even if, as Father Watson did, you stumble over a ten-gallon tin of creosote.

'I'm afraid I'm not accustomed to the poor light, Mrs James.'

'Look at the sky, father. Keep your eyes on the lightest part of the sky and they'll adapt little by little.'

Tilda had sprung ahead, at home in the dark, and anywhere within sight and sound of water. Feeling that she had given her due of politeness to the curate, the due exacted by her mother and elder sister, she pattered onto *Maurice*, and, after having a bit of a poke round, shot across the connecting gangplank onto *Grace*.

'You'll excuse me if I don't go any further, Mrs James. It's exactly what you said, it's the question of school attendance. The situation, you see, they tell me there's a legal aspect to it as well.'

How dispiriting for Father Watson to tell her this, Nenna thought, and how far it must be from his expectations when he received his first two minor orders, and made his last acts of resignation. To stand on this dusky wharf, bruised by a drum of creosote, and acting not even as the convent chaplain, but as some kind of school attendance officer!

'I know they haven't been coming to class regularly. But then, father, they haven't been well.'

Even Father Watson could scarcely be expected to swallow this. 'I was struck by the good health and spirits of your little one. In fact I had it in mind that she might be trained up to one of the women's auxiliary services which justified themselves so splendidly in the last war – the WRENS, I mean, of course. It's a service that's not incompatible with the Christian life.'

'You know how it is with children; she's well one day, not so well the next.' Nenna's attitude to truth was flexible, and more like Willis's than Richard's. 'And Martha's the same, it's only to be expected at her age.'

Nenna had hoped to alarm the curate with these references to approaching puberty, but he seemed, on the contrary, to be reassured. 'If that's the trouble, you couldn't do better than to entrust her to the skilled understanding of the Sisters.' How dogged he was. 'They'll expect, then, to see both your daughters in class on Monday next.'

'I'll do what I can.'

'Very well, Mrs James.'

'Won't you come as far as the boat?'

'No, no, I won't risk the crossing a second time.' What had happened the first time? 'And now, I'm afraid I've somewhat lost my sense of direction. I'll have to ask you my way to dry land.'

Nenna pointed out the way through the gate, which, swinging on its hinges, no longer provided any kind of barrier, out onto the Embankment, and first left, first right up Partisan Street for the King's Road. The priest couldn't have looked more relieved if he had completed a mission to those that dwell in the waters that are below the earth.

'I've got the supper, Ma,' said Martha, when Nenna returned to *Grace*. Nenna would have felt better pleased with herself if she had resembled her elder daughter. But Martha, small and thin, with dark eyes which already showed an acceptance of the world's shortcomings, was not like her mother and even less like her father. The crucial moment when children realise that their parents are younger than they are had long since been passed by Martha.

'We're having baked beans. If Father Watson's coming, we shall have to open another tin.'

'No, dear, he's gone home.'

Nenna felt tired, and sat down on the keelson, which ran from end to end of the flat-bottomed barge. It was quite wrong to come to depend too much upon one's children.

Martha set confidently to work in *Grace*'s galley, which

consisted of two gas rings in the bows connected to a Cálor cylinder, and a brass sink. Water came to the sink from a container on deck, which was refilled by a man from the boat-yard once every twenty-four hours. A good deal of improvisation was necessary and Martha had put three tin plates to heat up over the hissing saucepan of beans.

'Was it fun on *Lord Jim*?'

'Oh, not at all.'

'Should I have enjoyed it?'

'Oh no, I don't think so. Mrs Blake threw cheese straws into the stove.'

'What did Mr Blake say?'

'He wants to keep her happy, to make her happy, I don't know.'

'What did Father Watson want?'

'Didn't he talk to you at all?'

'I daresay he would have done, but I sent him out to fetch you, with Tilda, she needed exercise.'

'So he didn't mention anything.'

'He just came down here, and I made him a cup of tea and we said an act of contrition together.'

'He wanted to know why you hadn't been to class lately.'

Martha sighed.

'I've been reading your letters,' she said. 'They're lying about your cabin, and you haven't even looked at most of them.'

The letters were Nenna's connection, not only with the land, but with her previous existence. They would be from Canada, from her sister Louise who would suggest that she might put up various old acquaintances passing through London, or find a suitable family for a darling Austrian boy, not so very much older than Martha, whose father was a kind of Count, but was also in the import-export business, or try to recall a splendid person, the friend of a friend of hers who had had a very, very sad story. Then there were one or two bills, not many because Nenna had no credit accounts, a letter-card from an old schoolfriend which started Bet you don't remember me, and two charitable appeals, forwarded by Father Watson even to such an unpromising address as *Grace*.

'Anything from Daddy?'

'No, Ma, I looked for that first.'

There was no more to be said on that subject.

'Oh, Martha, my head aches. Baked beans would be just the thing for it.'

Tilda came in, wet, and black as coal from head to foot.

'Willis gave me a drawing.'

'What of?'

'*Lord Jim*, and some seagulls.'

'You shouldn't have accepted it.'

'Oh, I gave him one back.'

She had been waiting on *Dreadnought* to watch the water coming in through the main leak. It had come half way up the bunk, and nearly as far as Willis's blankets. Nenna was distressed.

'Well, it goes out with every tide. He'll have to show people round at low tide, and get them off before it turns.'

'Surely he can do some repairs,' said Martha.

'No, Fate's against him,' said Tilda, and after one or two forkfuls of beans she fell fast asleep with her head across the table. It was impossible, in any case, to bath her, because they were only allowed to let out the bathwater on a falling tide.

By now the flood was making fast. The mist had cleared, and to the north-east the Lots Road Power Station had discharged from its four majestic chimneys long plumes of white pearly smoke which slowly drooped and turned to dun. The lights dazzled, but on the broad face of the water there were innumerable V-shaped eddies, showing the exact position of whatever the river had not been able to hide. If the old Thames trades had still persisted, if boatmen had still made a living from taking the coins from the pockets of the drowned, then this was the hour for them to watch. Far above, masses of autumn cloud passed through the transparent violet sky.

After supper they sat by the light of the stove. Nenna was struck by the fact that she ought to write to Louise,

who was married to a successful business man. She began,
Dear Sis, Tell Joel that it's quite an education in itself for
the girls to be brought up in the heart of the capital, and
on the very shores of London's historic river.

2

TILDA was up aloft. *Grace*'s mast was fifteen foot of blackened pine, fitted into a tabernacle, so that it could be lowered to the deck in the days when *Grace* negotiated the twenty-eight tideway bridges between Richmond and the sea. Her mizzen mast was gone, her sprit was gone, the mainmast was never intended for climbing and Tilda sat where there was, apparently, nowhere to sit.

Martha, whose head was as strong as her sister's, sometimes climbed up as well, and, clinging on about a foot lower down, read aloud from a horror comic. But today Tilda was alone, looking down at the slanting angle of the decks as the cables gave or tightened, the passive shoreline, the secret water.

Tilda cared nothing for the future, and had, as a result, a great capacity for happiness. At the moment she was perfectly happy.

She was waiting for the tide to turn. Exactly opposite *Grace* a heap of crates which had driven up through the bends and reaches, twenty miles from Gravesend, was at rest in the slack water, enchanted apparently, not moving

an inch one way or the other. The lighters swung at
their moorings, pointing all ways, helpless without the
instructions of the tide. It was odd to see the clouds move
when the water was so still.

She blinked twice, taking the risk of missing the right
few seconds while her eyes were shut. Then one end of
a crate detached itself from the crates and began to steal
away, edging slowly round in a half circle. Tilda, who had
been holding her breath, let it go. A tremor ran through
the boats' cables, the iron lighters, just on the move,
chocked gently together. The great swing round began.
By the shore the driftwood was still travelling upriver, but
in midstream it was gathering way headlong in the other
direction. The Thames had turned towards the sea.

Willis had frequently told her that these old barges, in
spite of their great sails, didn't need a crew of more than
two men, in fact a man and a boy could handle them
easily. The sails had been tan-coloured, like the earth and
dressed with oil, which never quite dried out. There were
none left now. But *Grace* wouldn't need them to go out
to sea on the ebb tide. She wouldn't make sail until she
reached Port of London. With her flat bottom, she would
swim on the tide, all gear dropped, cunningly making
use of the hidden drifts. The six-year-old boy knew every
current and eddy of the river. Long had he studied the
secrets of the Thames. None but he would have noticed
the gleam of gold and diamonds – the ring on the dead

man's finger as his hand broke the surface. Farewell! He recognised it as the hand of his father, missing now for countless years. The *Grace*, 180 tons fully loaded, nosed her way through the low arches by the Middlesex bank, where there was no room for other craft, passing, or surpassing, all the shipping there. At Tower Bridge if four foot diameter discs bearing black and white signal stripes are displayed fourteen foot to landward of the signals, this is an indication that the bridge cannot be raised from mechanical or other cause. Only *Grace* could pass, not *Maurice*, not even *Dreadnought*, a sight never to be forgotten. Men and women came out on the dock to watch as the great brown sails went up, with only a six-year-old boy at the winch, and the *Grace*, bound for Ushant, smelled the open sea.

There was a scratching at the heel of the mast. A cat, with her mouth full of seagull feathers, was feebly trying to climb up, but after a few feet her claws lost purchase and she slithered back by gradual stages to the deck.

'Stripey!'

The ship's cat was in every way appropriate to the Reach. She habitually moved in a kind of nautical crawl, with her stomach close to the deck, as though close-furled and ready for dirty weather. The ears were vestigial, and lay flat to the head.

Through years of attempting to lick herself clean, for she had never quite lost her self-respect, Stripey had become as thickly coated with mud inside as out. She was in a perpetual process of readjustment, not only to tides and seasons, but to the rats she encountered on the wharf. Up to a certain size, that is to say the size attained by the rats at a few weeks old, she caught and ate them, and, with a sure instinct for authority, brought in their tails to lay them at the feet of Martha. Any rats in excess of this size chased Stripey. The resulting uncertainty as to whether she was coming or going had made her, to some extent, mentally unstable.

Stripey did not care to be fed by human beings, and understood how to keep herself warm in cold weather. She slept outside, on one or other of the stove pipes which projected out of the stacks on deck. Curled up on the pipe, she acted as an obstruction which drove the smoke down again into the barge, making it almost uninhabitable. In turn, Woodie, Willis, Nenna, Maurice and even his visitors could be heard coughing uncontrollably. But Stripey rarely chose to sleep in the same place two nights running.

From the masthead Tilda, having sailed out to sea with *Grace*, took a closer survey of the Reach. Her whole idea of the world's work was derived from what she observed there and had little in common with the circulation of the great city which toiled on only a hundred yards away.

No movement on *Lord Jim*. Willis was walking towards

Dreadnought with the man from the boatyard, whose manner suggested that he was refusing to supply more tar, gas and water until the previous bill had been paid.

On *Rochester*, Woodie was getting ready to lay up for the winter. It seemed that he was not, after all, a true barge-dweller. His small recording company, as he explained only too often, had gone into voluntary liquidation, leaving him with just enough to manage nicely, and he was going to spend the cold weather in his house in Purley. Managing nicely seemed an odd thing to do at the north end of the Reach. Woodie also spoke of getting someone to anti-foul his hull, so that it would be as clean as *Lord Jim*'s. The other barges were so deeply encrusted with marine life that it was difficult to strike wood. Green weeds and barnacles were thick on them, and whales might have saluted them in passing.

Maurice was deserted, Maurice having been invited, as he quite often was, to go down for the day to Brighton. But his deckhouse did not appear to be locked. A light van drew up on the wharf, and a man got out and dropped a large quantity of cardboard boxes over the side of the wharf onto the deck. One of them broke open. It was full of hair-dryers. The man then had to drop down on deck and arrange the boxes more carefully. It would have been better to cover them with a tarpaulin, but he had forgotten to bring one, perhaps. He wasted no time in looking round and it was only when he was backing the van to drive away that his face could be seen. It was very pale and had no expression, as though expressions were surplus to requirements.

Willis, walking in his deliberate way, looked at the boxes on *Maurice*, paused, even shook his head a little, but did nothing. Nenna might have added to her list of things that men do better than women their ability to do nothing at all in an unhurried manner. And in fact there was nothing that Willis could do about the boxes. Quite certainly, *Maurice* did not want the police on his boat.

'Ahoy there, Tilda! Watch yourself!' Willis called.

Tilda knew very well that the river could be dangerous. Although she had become a native of the boats, and pitied the tideless and ratless life of the Chelsea inhabitants, she respected the water and knew that one could die within sight of the Embankment.

One spring evening a Dutch barge, the *Waalhaven*, from Rotterdam, glittering with brass, impressive, even under power, had anchored in midstream opposite the boats. She must have got clearance at Gravesend and sailed up on the ebb. Of this fine vessel the *Maurice*, also from Rotterdam, had once been a poor relation. The grounded barges seemed to watch the *Waalhaven*, as prisoners watch the free.

Her crew lined up on deck as gravely as if at a business meeting. A spotless meeting of well-regarded business men in rubber seaboots, conducted in the harmonious spirit which had always characterised the firm.

Just after teatime the owner came to the rails and called out to *Maurice* to send a dinghy so that he could put a party ashore. When nothing happened, and he realised that he had come to a place without facilities, he retired for another consultation. Then, as the light began to fail, with the tide running very fast, three of them launched their own dinghy and prepared to sail to the wharf. They had been waiting for high water so that they could sail alongside in a civilised manner. It was like a demonstration in small boat sailing, a lesson in holiday sport. They still wore their seaboots, but brought their shoregoing shoes with them in an oilskin bag. The gods of the river had, perhaps, taken away their wits.

The offshore wind was coming hard as usual through the wide gap between the warehouses on the Surrey side. Woodie, observing their gallant start, longed to lend them his Chart 3 and to impress upon them that there was one competent owner at least at this end of the Reach. Richard, back from work after a tiresome day, stopped on the Embankment to look, and remembered that he had once gone on board the *Waalhaven* for a drink when she put in at Orfordness.

Past the gap, the wind failed and dropped to nothing, the dinghy lost way and drifted towards three lighters moored abreast. Her mast caught with a crack which could be heard on both sides of the river on the high overhang of the foremost lighter. The whole dinghy was jammed and sucked in under the stem, then rolled over, held fast by her steel mast which would not snap. The men were pitched overboard and they too were swallowed up beneath the heavy iron bottoms of the lighters. After a while the bag of shoes came up, then two of the men, then a pair of seaboots, floating soles upwards.

Tilda thought of this incident with distress, but not often. She wondered what had happened to the other pairs of boots. But her heart did not rule her memory, as was the case with Martha and Nenna. She was spared that inconvenience.

Willis called again, 'Ahoy there, Tilda! Don't shout down back to me!' Imagining her to be delicate, he was anxious for her not to strain her voice. Tilda and Martha both sang absolutely true, and Willis, who was fond of music, and always optimistic about the future of others, liked to think of them as concert performers. They could still manage *Abends, wenn wir schlafen gehen*, taught them by the nuns as a party piece, and then, indeed, they sounded like angels, though angels without much grasp of the words after the second line. More successful, perhaps, was *Jailhouse Rock*. But Tilda had taught herself to produce, by widening her mouth into the shape of an oblong, a most unpleasant imitation of a bosun's whistle, which could be heard almost as far as *Lord Jim*. The sound indicated that she was coming down the mast. Father Watson had been more than a little frightened by it, and had confided in the nuns that it was more like something produced by some mechanical contrivance, than by a human being. His words confirmed the opinion of the Sisters of Misericord that the two children, so clever and musical, were at risk on the boat, spiritually and perhaps physically, and that someone ought to speak much more seriously to Mrs James.

3

BELOW decks, *Grace* was shipshape, but after calling on *Lord Jim* Nenna always felt impelled to start cleaning the brightwork. They hadn't much — just the handholds of the companion, the locker hinges, and the pump-handle of the heads, which was part of the original equipment and was engraved with the date: 1905.

Nenna was thirty-two, an age by which if a blonde woman's hair hasn't turned dark, it never will. She had come to London after the war as a music student, and felt by this time she was neither Canadian nor English. Edward and she had got married in 1949. She was still at the RSM then, violin first study, and she fell in love as only a violinist can. She didn't know if they had given themselves sufficient time to think things over before they married — that was the kind of question her sister Louise asked. Edward stayed in the Engineers for a bit, then came out and was not very successful in finding a job to suit him. That wasn't his fault, and if anyone said that it was, Nenna would still feel like poking a hole in them. They got a flat. People who asked her why she didn't make use

of her talent and give singing lessons had perhaps not tried
to do this while living in two rooms over a greengrocer's,
and looking after young children. But Edward was said
by his friends to have business sense, and to be able to
make things work. That was why the launderette was so
evidently a good investment. It was quite a new idea over
here, you didn't do your washing at home but brought
it out to these machines, and the courteous manager
greeted you and put in the soap powder for you, and
had the clothes all ready for you when you came back,
but wasn't alas, as it turned out, much of a hand at doing
the accounts. The closing of the launderette had given rise
to a case in the County Court, in which Edward and she
had been held not to blame, but had been conscious of
the contempt of their solicitor, who always seemed to be
in a great hurry.

This, no doubt, was the reason that Nenna's thoughts,
whenever she was alone, took the form of a kind of
perpetual magistrates' hearing, in which her own version
of her marriage was shown as ridiculously simple and
demonstrably right, and then, almost exactly at the
same time, as incontrovertibly wrong. Her conscience,
too, held, quite uninvited, a separate watching brief, and
intervened in the proceedings to read statements of an
unwelcome nature.

'. . . Your life story so far, Mrs James, has had a certain
lack of distinction. I dare say it seemed distinguished

enough while you were living it – distinguished, at least, from other peoples' lives.'

'You put that very well, my lord.' She realised that the magistrate had become a judge.

'Now then ... in 1959 your husband came to the conclusion, and I am given to understand that you fully agreed, that it would be a sensible step for him to take employment for fifteen months with a construction firm in Central America, in order to save the larger part of his salary ...'

Nenna protested that she had never exactly thought it sensible, it was the parting of lovers, which must always be senseless, but they'd both of them thought that David, Panama, would be a wretched place to take small children to. The words sounded convincing, the judge leaned forward in approbation. Encouraged, she admitted that she had been entrusted with their last £2000, and had bought a houseboat, in point of fact, the barge *Grace*.

'The children missed their father?'

'The older one did. Tilda didn't seem to, but no-one understands what she thinks except Martha.'

'Thank you, Mrs James, we should like you to confine yourself to first-hand evidence ... you wrote to your husband, of course, to explain the arrangements you had made in his absence?'

'I gave him our new address at once. Of course I did.'

'The address you gave him was 626 Cheyne Walk, Chelsea SW10?'

'Yes, that's right. That's the address of the boatyard office, where they take in the letters.'

'. . . giving him the impression, as indeed it would to anyone who did not know the district, that you had secured a well-appointed house or flat in Chelsea, at a very reasonable figure?'

'Well-appointed' was quite unfair, but Nenna's defence, always slow to move, failed to contest it.

'I didn't want to worry him. And then, plenty of people would give a lot to live on the Reach.'

'You are shifting your ground, Mrs James . . .'

'When I sent photographs to my sister in Canada, she thought it looked beautiful.'

'The river is thought of as romantic?'

'Yes, that's so!'

'More so by those who do not know it well?'

'I can't answer that.'

'They may be familiar with the paintings of Whistler, or perhaps with Whistler's statement that when evening mist clothes the riverside with poetry, as with a veil, and the poor buildings lose themselves in the dim sky, and the tall chimneys become campanili, and the warehouses are palaces in the night, and the whole city hangs in the heavens, and fairyland is before us — then the wayfarer hastens home, and Nature, who, for once, has sung in tune, sings her exquisite song to the artist alone, her son and her master – her son, in that he loves her, her master in that he knows her?' . . . shall I read you that deposition again, Mrs James?'

Nenna was silent.

'Whistler, however, lived in a reasonably comfortable house?'

Nenna refused to give way. 'You soon get used to the little difficulties. Most people like it very much.'

'Mrs James. Did your husband, on his return to this country, where he expected to be reunited with his wife and family, like the houseboat *Grace* very much?'

'A number of these houseboats, or disused barges, including *Grace*, are exceedingly damp?'

'Mrs James. Do you like your husband?'

'Mrs James. Did your husband, or did he not, complain that the houseboat *Grace*, apart from being damp, needed extensive repairs, and that it was difficult if not impossible for you to resume any meaningful sexual relationship when your cabin acted as a kind of passageway with your daughters constantly going to and fro to gain access to the hatch, and a succession of persons, including the milkman, trampling overhead? You will tell me that the milkman has refused to continue deliveries, but this only adds weight to my earlier submission that the boat is not only unfit to live in but actually unsafe.'

'I love him, I want him. While he was away was the longest fifteen months and eight days I ever spent. I can't believe even now that it's over. Why don't I go to him? Well, why doesn't he come to us? He hasn't found anywhere at all that we could all of us live together. He's in some kind of rooms in the north-east of London somewhere.'

'42b Milvain Street, Stoke Newington.'

'In Christ's name, who's ever heard of such a place?'

'Have you made any effort to go and see the plaintiff there, Mrs James? I must remind you that we cannot admit any second-hand evidence.'

So now it was out. She was the defendant, or rather the accused, and should have known it all along.

'I repeat. Have you ever been to Milvain Street, which, for all any of us know, may be a perfectly suitable home for yourself and the issue of the marriage?'

'I know it isn't. How can it be?'

'Is he living there by himself?'

'I'm pretty sure so.'

'Not with another woman?'

'He's never mentioned one.'

'In his letters?'

'He's never liked writing letters very much.'

'But you write to him every day. That is perhaps too often?'

'It seems I can't do right. Everyone knows that women write a lot of letters.'

To the disapproval and distaste of the court she was shouting.

'I only want him to give way a little. I only want him to say that I've done well in finding somewhere for us to be!'

'You are very dependent on praise, Mrs James.'

'That depends, my lord, on who it's from.'

'You could be described as an obstinate bitch?' That was an intervention from her conscience but she had never been known for obstinacy in the past, and it was puzzling to account, really, for her awkward persistence about *Grace*. In calmer moments, too, she understood how it was that Edward, though generous at heart, found it difficult to give way. He was not much used to giving at all. His family, it seemed, had not been in the habit of exchanging presents, almost inconceivably to Nenna, whose childhood had been gift-ridden, with much atonement, love and reconciliation conveyed in the bright wrappings. Edward had no idea of how to express himself in that way. Nor was he fortunate as a shopper. He had realised, for instance, when Martha was born, that he would do well to take flowers to the hospital, but not that if you buy an azalea in winter and carry it on a bus and through a number of cold streets, all the buds will drop off before you arrive.

Nenna had never criticised the bloomless azalea. It was the other young mothers in the beds each side of her who had laughed at it. That had been 1951. Two of the new babies in the ward had been christened Festival.

'Your attention, Mrs James.'

The first exhibit in her case was a painful quarrel, laid out before the court in its naked entirety. Edward had not come back from the construction firm at David with anything saved up, but then, she had hardly expected him to. If he had saved anything he would have changed character and would hardly have been the man she loved. And, after all, they had *Grace*. Nenna, who was of hopeful temperament, intended to ask Edward's mother to look after Martha and Tilda for a while. She and Edward would be alone on *Grace*, and they could batten down and stay in bed for twenty-four hours if they felt like it.

'Mrs James, are you asking the court to believe that you were sincere in this? You know perfectly well that your husband's mother lives at a considerable distance, in point of fact in a suburb of Sheffield, and that she has never at any time offered to look after your children.'

Edward had made the same objection. And yet this particular quarrel, now that it was under rigorous scrutiny, hadn't arisen over that matter at all, but over something else entirely, the question of where Nenna could possibly have put his squash racquets while he was away. They had both of them thought that the climate of Panama would be bad for the racquets, although it turned out in the end that he could perfectly well have taken them with him. If Nenna had brought them with her to *Grace*, they must certainly have been ruined by the damp. But, worse still, they were not on *Grace*. Nenna was full of contrition. O my God, I am heartily sorry for having offended Thee. Thirty minutes of squash gives a man as much exercise as two hours of any other game. She had been entrusted with the racquets. They were, in a sense, a sacred trust. But she could not remember anything at all about them.

'You mislaid them deliberately?'

'I don't do anything deliberately.'

That seemed to be true. Some of her actions were defensive, others optimistic, more than half of them mistaken.

'On this occasion you lost your temper, and threw a solid object at Mr James?'

It had only been her bank book, and Edward had been quite right to say that it was not worth reading.

But then the exhibit, the quarrel, hateful and confusing in being exposed to other eyes, changed character and became after all, evidence for the defence. In mid-fury Edward had asked what day of the week she imagined it was, for at the time, in the highly coloured world of the argument, this detail had become of supreme importance.

'Look here, is it Wednesday or Thursday?'

'I don't know, Ed, whichever you like.'

Given so much free choice, he had melted immediately, and by good fortune they had several hours alone on the boat. The girls were at school, and no misery that Nenna had ever felt could weigh against their happiness which flowed like the current, with its separate eddies, of the strong river beneath them.

Perhaps the whole case was breaking down, to the disappointment of the advocates, who, after all, could hardly be distinguished from the prosecution on both sides. So little was needed for a settlement, and yet the word 'settlement' suggested two intractable people, and they were both quite humble. Nor was it true, as their accusers impartially suggested, that she or Edward preferred to live in an atmosphere of crisis. They both needed peace and turned in memory towards their peaceful moments together, finding their true home there.

When Nenna was not in the witness box, she sometimes saw herself getting ready for an inspection at which Edward, or Edward's mother, or some power superior to either, gave warning that they might appear — she could only hope that it would be on a falling tide — to see where she could be found wanting. Determined not to fail this test, she let the image fade into the business of polishing the brasses and cleaning ship. The decks must be clear, hatches fastened, Stripey out of sight, and above all the girls ought to be back in regular education.

'You're both going in to school on Monday, aren't you, Martha?'

Martha, like her father, and like Richard, saw no need for fictions. She gave her mother a dark brown, level glance.

'I shall go in, and take Tilda with me, when the situation warrants it.'

'We shall have Father Watson round again.'

'I don't think so, Ma. He missed his footing on the gangplank last time.'

'I'm so tired of making excuses.'

'You should tell the truth.'

In what way could the truth be made acceptable? Tilda had initiated the train of events, as, with her careless mastery of life, she often did. Pressed by the nuns to complete a kettleholder in cross-stitch as a present for her father, she had replied that she had never seen her father holding a kettle and that Daddy had gone away.

The fact was that she had lost the six square inches of canvas allocated for the kettleholder when it was first given out to the class. Martha knew this, but did not wish to betray her sister.

Tilda had at first elaborated her story, saying that her mother was looking for a new Daddy, but her observation, quick as a bird's flight, showed her that this was going too far, and she added that she and her sister prayed nightly to Our Lady of Fatima for her father's return. Up till that moment Tilda, in spite of her lucid grey eyes, showing clarity beneath clarity, which challenged the nuns not to risk scandalising the innocent, had often been in disfavour. She was known to be one of the little ones who had filled in their colouring books irreverently, making our Lord's beard purple, or even green, largely, to be sure, because she never bothered to get hold of the best crayons first. Now, however, she was the object of compassion. After a private conference with Mother Superior, the Sisters announced that there would be a special rosary every morning, during the time set aside for special intentions, and that the whole Junior School would pray together that Martha and Tilda's Daddy should come back to them. After this, if the weather was fine, there would be a procession to the life size model of the grotto of Lourdes, which had been built in the recreation ground out of a kind of artificial rock closely resembling anthracite. Sister Paul, who was the author of several devotional volumes, wrote the special prayer: Heart of Jesus, grant that the eyes of the non-Catholic father of Thy little servants, Martha and Matilda, may be opened, that his tepid soul may become fervent, and that he may return to establish himself on his rightful hearth, Amen.

'They are good women,' Martha said, 'but I'm not going to set foot in the place while that's going on.'

'I could speak to the nuns.'

'I'd rather you didn't, Ma. They might begin to pray for you as well.'

She glanced up, apparently casually, to see if Nenna had taken this too hard.

Tilda appeared with a ball of oozing clay in her arms which she flung down on the table. Apparently carrion, it moved and stretched a lean back leg, which turned out to be Stripey's.

'She's in voluntary liquidation,' said Martha, but she fetched a piece of old towelling and began to rub the cat, which squinted through the folds of white material like Lazarus through the grave-clothes.

'How did she get into this state?' Nenna asked. 'That isn't shore mud.'

'She was hunting rats on the wharf and she fell into a clay lighter, Mercantile Lighterage Limited, flag black diamond on broad white band.'

'Who brought her in, then?'

'One of the lightermen got off at Cadogan Stairs and walked back with her and gave her to Maurice.'

'Well, try to squeeze the water out of her tail. Gently.'

The clay rapidly set in a hard surface on the table and the floorboards underneath it. Martha mopped and scraped away for almost half an hour, long after Tilda had lost interest. During this time it grew dark, the darkness seeming to rise from the river to make it one with the sky. Nenna made the tea and lit the wood stove. The old barges, who had once beaten their way up and down the East Coast and the Channel ports, grumbled and heaved at their cables while their new owners sat back in peace.

Without warning, a shaft of brilliant light, in colour a sickly mauve, shone down the hatchway.

'It must be from *Maurice*,' said Martha, 'it can't be a shore light.'

They could hear his footsteps across the gangplank, then a heavier one as he dropped the eighteen-inch gap onto *Grace*'s deck.

'Maurice can't weigh much. He just springs about.'

'Cat-like?' Nenna asked.

'Heaven forbid,' said Martha.

'*Grace!*' Maurice called, in imitation of Richard, 'perhaps you'd like to come and have a look.'

Nenna and the two girls shook off a certain teatime drowsiness and went back on deck, where they stood astounded. On the afterdeck of *Maurice*, which lay slightly at an angle to *Grace*, a strange transformation had taken place. The bright light – this was what had struck them first – issued from an old street lamp, leaning at a crazy angle, rather suggesting an amateur production of *Tales of Hoffmann*, fitted, in place of glass, with sheets of mauve plastic, and trailing a long cable which disappeared down the companion. On the deck itself were scattered what looked like paving stones, and the leeboard winch had been somewhat garishly painted in red, white, and gold.

The wash of a passing collier rocked both boats and the enormous reverberation of her wailing hooter filled the air and made it impossible for them to speak. Maurice stood half in the shadow, half brightly purple, and at last was able to say.

'It'll make you think of Venice, won't it?'

Nenna hesitated.

'I've never been to Venice.'

'Nor have I,' said Maurice, quick to disclaim any pretence to superiority, 'I got the idea from a postcard someone sent me. Well, he sent me quite a series of postcards, and from them I was able to reconstruct a typical street corner. Not the Grand Canal, you understand, just one of the little ones. When it's as warm as it is tonight, you'll be able to leave the hatch open and imagine yourselves in the heart of Venice.'

'It's beautiful!' Tilda shouted.

'You don't seem quite certain about it, Nenna.'

'I am, I am. I've always wanted to see Venice, almost more than any other place. I was only wondering what would happen when the wind gets up.'

What she must not ask, but at the same time mustn't be thought not to be asking, was what would happen when Harry came next. As a depot for stolen goods *Maurice*, surely, had to look as inconspicuous as possible.

'I may be going abroad myself quite soon,' said Maurice casually.

'Oh, you didn't tell us.'

'Yes, I met someone the other night who made a sort of suggestion about a possible job of some kind.'

It wasn't worth asking of what kind; there had been so many beginnings. Sometimes Maurice went over to Bayswater to keep up his skating, in the hopes of getting a job in the ice show. Perhaps it was that he was talking about now.

'Would you be selling *Maurice*, then?'

'Oh yes, of course, when I go abroad.'

'Well, your leak isn't nearly as bad as *Dreadnought*.'

This practical advice seemed to depress Maurice, who was trying the paving stones in various positions.

'I must ask Willis how he's getting on . . . there's so much to think about . . . if someone wanted a description of this boat, I suppose the Venetian corner would be a feature . . .'

He switched off the mauve light. None of the barge-owners could afford to waste electricity, and the display was really intended for much later at night, but he had turned it on early to surprise and please them.

'Yes! I'll soon be living on land. I shall tell my friend to take all his bits and pieces out of my hold, of course.'

'Maurice is going mad,' said Martha, quietly, as they went back onto *Grace*.

4

MAURICE'S strange period of hopefulness did not last
long. Tenderly responsive to the self-deceptions of others,
he was unfortunately too well able to understand his
own. No more was said of the job and it rapidly became
impossible to tell who was trying to please whom over
the matter of the Venetian lantern.

'What am I to do, Maurice?' Nenna asked. She confided
in him above all others. Apart from anything else, his
working day did not begin till seven or eight, so that
he was often there during the day, and always ready
to listen; but there were times when his customers left
early, at two or three in the morning, and then Maurice,
somewhat exhilarated with whisky, would come over to
Grace, magically retaining his balance on the gangplank,
and sit on the gunwale, waiting. He never went below,
for fear of disturbing the little girls. Nenna used to wrap
up in her coat and bring out two rugs for him.

During the small hours, tipsy Maurice became an
oracle, ambiguous, wayward, but impressive. Even his
voice changed a little. He told the sombre truths of

the lighthearted, betraying in a casual hour what was never intended to be shown. If the tide was low the two of them watched the gleams on the foreshore, at half tide they heard the water chuckling, waiting to lift the boats, at flood tide they saw the river as a powerful god, bearded with the white foam of detergents, calling home the twenty-seven lost rivers of London, sighing as the night declined.

'Maurice, ought I to go away?'

'You can't.'

'You said you were going to go away yourself.'

'No-one believed it. You didn't. What do the others think?'

'They think your boat belongs to Harry.'

'Nothing belongs to Harry, certainly all that stuff in the hold doesn't. He finds it easier to live without property. As to *Maurice*, my godmother gave me the money to buy a bit of property when I left Southport.'

'I've never been to Southport.'

'It's very nice. You take the train from the middle of Liverpool, and it's the last station, right out by the seaside.'

'Have you been back since?'

'No.'

'If *Maurice* belongs to you, why do you have to put up with Harry?'

'I can't answer that.'

'What will you do if the police come?'

'What will you do if your husband doesn't?'

Nenna thought, I must take the opportunity to get things settled for me, even if it's only by chance, like throwing straws into the current. She repeated –

'Maurice, what shall I do?'

'Well, have you been to see him yet?'

'Not yet. But of course I ought to. As soon as I can find someone to stay with the girls, for a night or two if it's necessary, I'm going to go. Thank you for making my mind up.'

'No, don't do that.'

'Don't do what?'

'Don't thank me.'

'Why not?'

'Not for that.'

'But, you know, by myself I can't make my mind up.'

'You shouldn't do it at all.'

'Why not, Maurice?'

'Why should you think it's a good thing to do? Why should it make you any happier? There isn't one kind of happiness, there's all kinds. Decision is torment for anyone with imagination. When you decide, you multiply the things you might have done and now never can. If there's even one person who might be hurt by a decision, you should never make it. They tell you, make up your mind or it will be too late, but if it's really too late, we should be grateful. You know very well that we're two of the same kind, Nenna. It's right for us to live where we do, between land and water. You, my dear, you're half in love with your husband, then there's Martha who's half a child and half a girl, Richard who can't give up being half in the Navy, Willis who's half an artist and half a longshoreman, a cat who's half alive and half dead . . .'

He stopped before describing himself, if, indeed, he had been going to do so.

Partisan Street, opposite the Reach, was a rough place, well used to answering police enquiries. The boys looked on the Venetian corner as a godsend and came every day as soon as they were out of school to throw stones at it. After a week Harry returned to *Maurice*, once again when there was no-one on the boat, took away his consignment of hair-dryers, and threw the lantern and the paving-stones overboard. Tilda, an expert mudlark, retrieved most of the purple plastic, but the pieces were broken and it was hard to see what could be done with them. Maurice appreciated the thought, but seemed not to care greatly one way or the other.

5

WILLIS deeply respected Richard, whom he privately thought of, and sometimes called aloud, the Skipper. Furthermore, although he had been pretty well openly accused of dishonesty at the meeting, his moral standards were much the same as Richard's, only he did not feel he was well enough off to apply them as often, and in such a wide range of conditions, as the Skipper. It didn't, thank heavens, seem likely that a situation would ever arise in which there was no hope for Richard, whereas, on the other hand, Willis considered that for himself there was scarcely any hope at all if he could not sell *Dreadnought*. £2000 would, according to his calculations, be more or less enough for him to go and spend the rest of his days with his widowed sister. He could hardly go empty-handed, and the benefits of the move had been pointed out to him often.

'My sister's place is on gravel soil. You don't feel the damp there. Couldn't feel it if you wanted to.'

Nor, however, did you see the river, and Willis would have to find something else to fill the great gap which would be left in his life when it was no longer possible to see the river traffic, passing and repassing. Like many marine painters he had never been to sea. During the war he had been an auxiliary coastguard. He knew nothing about blue water sailing. But to sit still and watch while the ships proceeded on their lawful business, to know every class, every rig and every cargo, is to make inactivity a virtue, and Willis from *Dreadnought* and from points along the shore as far as the Cat and Lobster at Gravesend had honourably conducted the profession of looking on. Born in Silvertown, within sound of the old boat-builders' yards, he disliked silence. Like Tilda, he found it easier to sleep when he could hear the lighters, like iron coffins on Resurrection Day, clashing each other at their moorings all night, and behind that the whisper of shoal water.

Tilda, in spite of her lack of success with the convent's colouring books, wished to be a marine painter also. Her object was to paint exactly like Willis, and to put in all the rigging with a ruler, and to get everything right. She also wanted to have a Sunday dinner, whenever possible, in the style of Willis, who followed the bargemen's custom of serving first sultana pudding with gravy, and then the roast.

As an artist, he had always made an adequate living, and Willises, carefully packed in stiff board and oiled paper, were despatched – since a number of his patrons were in the Merchant Navy – to ports all over the world for collection. But these commissions, mostly for the originals of jokes and cartoons which Willis had managed in former times to sell to magazines, had grown fewer and fewer in the last ten years, as, indeed, had the drawings themselves. After the war the number of readers who would laugh at pictures of seasick passengers, or bosuns getting the better of the second mate, diminished rapidly.

A few distant correspondents, untouched by time, still asked confidently for a painting of a particular ship. *Dear Willis — As I am informed by those who ought to know that you have 'taken the ground' somewhere near London River, I expect you can tell me the whereabouts of the dear old* Fortuna, *built 1892, rigged when I last saw her in 1920 as a square foresail brigantine. Old ships never die and doubtless she is still knocking around the East Coast, though I suppose old Payne may have made his last port by now . . . I should be interested in an oil painting on canvas, or board (which I suppose would come a bit cheaper!!), showing her beating around the Foreland under sail in fairly heavy weather, say Force 6 . . .* Willis could only pray that the writers of such letters, stranded in ports which the war had passed by almost without notice, would never return, to be betrayed by so much change.

Willis sometimes took Tilda, in her character as an apprentice painter, to the Tate Gallery, about two and a half miles along the Embankment. There was no Tube then to Pimlico, and they proceeded by a series of tacks to Victoria. At Sloane Square Underground Station Willis pointed out the mighty iron pipe crossing high in the air above the passenger line.

'Look, that carries the River Westbourne, flowing down from Paddington. If that was to take and start leaking, we'd all have to swim for it.'

Tilda eyed the great pipe.

'Where does it come out?'

'The outfall? Well, it's one of the big sewers, my dear, I'll get the name right for you.' He made a note.

The other passengers drew back from the dishevelled river dwellers, so far out of their element.

Laura was doubtful whether the little girl ought to be allowed to go out like that alone with an old man, and not a very scrupulous one at that, for a whole afternoon. She told Richard a number of stories on the subject, some of them taken from the daily papers, and suggested that he might turn the matter over in his mind. But Richard said it wasn't necessary.

'You told me yourself that he was dishonest.'

'It isn't necessary.'

Willis and Tilda usually stopped on the way at a little shop in the Vauxhall Bridge Road, which seemed glad of any kind of custom, to buy a quarter of aniseed marbles. These were sold loose, but were put into a special paper bag overprinted with the words

COME ON, CHILDREN, HERE'S A NEW HIT!
FIRST YOU ROLL IT, THEN YOU CHEW IT.

Willis had never known many children, and until Nenna

had come to the boats he had rather tended to forget there were such things. The very distinctive taste of the aniseed marbles, which were, perhaps, some of the nastiest sweets ever made, recovered time past for him.

Once at the Tate, they usually had time only to look at the sea and river pieces, the Turners and the Whistlers. Willis praised these with the mingled pride and humility of an inheritor, however distant. To Tilda, however, the fine pictures were only extensions of her life on board. It struck her as odd, for example, that Turner, if he spent so much time on Chelsea Reach, shouldn't have known that a seagull always alights on the highest point. Well aware that she was in a public place, she tried to modify her voice; only then Willis didn't always hear, and she had to try again a good deal louder.

'Did Whistler do that one?'

The attendant watched her, hoping that she would get a little closer to the picture, so that he could relieve the boredom of his long day by telling her to stand back.

'What did he put those two red lights up there for? They're for obstruction not completely covered by water, aren't they? What are they doing there among the riding lights?'

'They don't miss much, do they?' the attendant said to Willis. 'I mean, your little granddaughter there.'

The misunderstanding delighted Tilda, 'Dear grandfather, are you sure you are not weary? Let us return to our ship. Take my arm, for though I am young, I am strong.'

Willis dealt with her admirably by taking almost no notice of what she said.

'Whistler was a very good painter. You don't want to make any mistake about that. It's only amateurs who think he isn't. There's Old Battersea Bridge. That was the old wooden bridge. Painted on a grey ground, you see, to save himself trouble. Tide on the turn, lighter taking advantage of the ebb.'

It was understood that on their return they would have tea on *Grace*.

'How old do you think I am, Mrs James?' Willis asked, leaning quietly forward. 'Don't tell me you've never thought about it. It's my experience that everybody thinks how old everybody else is.'

There was no help for it. 'Well, perhaps nearer seventy than sixty.'

Willis's expression never changed quickly. It seemed to be a considerable undertaking for him to rearrange the leathery brown cheeks and the stiff grey eyebrows which were apparently supported by his thick-lensed spectacles.

'I don't seem to feel my age while I'm on these little expeditions, or when I'm drawing.'

Now he wouldn't have time for either. Cleaning ship, and worrying about the visits of intending purchasers, occupied his entire horizon.

His ideas proceeded from simplicity to simplicity. If the main leak could be concealed by showing only at low tide, Willis thought that the equally serious problem of rain − for the weatherboards were particularly weak in one place − could be solved if he stood directly under the drip, wearing a sort of broad waterproof hat. He was sure he had one stowed away somewhere.

'He's no idea of how to sell anything except his drawings,' Woodie told Charles, 'and then I doubt whether he charges enough for them. I should describe him as an innocent.'

'He knows a fair amount about boats.'

'He lives in the past. He was asking me about some man called Payne who seems to have died years ago.'

Richard saw, with reservations, where his duty lay, and put *Dreadnought* on the market through the agency of an old RNVR friend of his, who had gone into partnership, on coming out of the forces, as an estate agent in Halkin Street. Perhaps 'acquaintance' would be a fairer description than 'friend', but the difference was clearer in peacetime than it had been during the war.

The agent was up-to-date and wished, as was fashionable in those years, to give an amusing turn to the advertisement, which he thought ought to appear, not where Willis had thought of putting it, in the *Exchange and Mart*, but in the A circulation newspapers.

'. . . Whistler's Battersea . . . main water . . . no? well, main electricity . . . two cabins, one suitable for a tiny Flying Dutchman . . . huge Cutty Sark type hold awaits conversion . . . complete with resident Ancient Mariner . . . might be persuaded to stop awhile if you splice the mainbrace . . .'

The senior partner usually drafted these announcements himself, but all the partners felt that, given the chance, they could do it better.

'The *Cutty Sark* was a tea clipper,' Richard said. 'And I don't think there's any question of Willis staying on board. In fact, that's really the whole point of the transaction.'

'Did this barge go to Dunkirk?'

'A number of them were drafted,' Richard said, '*Grace* was, and *Maurice*, but not *Dreadnought*, I think.'

'Pity. It would have been a selling point. How would it be, Richard, if we were to continue this discussion over a very large pink gin?'

This remark, often repeated, had earned Richard's friend, or acquaintance, the nickname of Pinkie.

Since this meeting, Richard had had a further debate with his conscience. It was, of course, the purchaser's business to employ a surveyor, whether a house or a boat was in question, and Pinkie would not be offering *Dreadnought* with any kind of guarantee as to soundness, only, after all, as to quaintness. On the other hand, Pinkie seemed to have lost his head to a certain extent, perhaps at the prospect of making his mark by bringing in something novel in the way of business. Surely he hadn't been quite so irritating as a watchkeeping officer in the *Lanark*? But the weakest element in the situation – the one most in need of protection, towards which Richard would always return – the weakest element was certainly Willis. He had begun to neglect himself, Laura said. She had gone along once to pay a casual visit and found one of Nenna's youngsters, the little one, cooking some kind of mess for him in *Dreadnought*'s galley. Richard rather liked Willis's pictures, and had got him to do a pen and wash drawing of *Lord Jim*. He saw the old man as in need of what, by current standards, was a very small sum to enable him to wind up his affairs.

Richard was not aware that he was no longer reasoning, but allowing a series of overlapping images – the drawing of *Lord Jim*, Tilda cooking – to act as a substitute for argument, so that his mind was working in a way not far different from Maurice's, or Nenna's. But the end product would be very different – not indecisive and multiple, but single and decisive. Without this faculty of Richard's, the world could not be maintained in its present state.

Having explained carefully to Willis what he was about to do, Richard invited Pinkie out to lunch. This had to be at a restaurant, because the only club that Richard belonged to was Pratt's. He had got himself put up for Pratt's because it was impossible to have lunch there.

There was, too, something unaccountable about Richard
– perhaps the same wilfulness that induced him to live
offshore although his marriage was in a perilous state –
which attracted him to Pratt's because celebrations were
only held there for the death of a king or queen.

The restaurant to which Richard invited Pinkie was one
at which he had an account, and there was, at least, no
difficulty in knowing what drinks to order. Pinkie sucked
in his drink in a curious manner, very curious considering
how many gins he must have in the course of the week, as
though his glass was a blowhole in Arctic ice and to drink
was his only hope of survival.

'By the way, Richard, when are you and Laura going
to give up this nonsense about living in the middle of the
Thames? This is the moment to acquire property, I'm sure
you realise that.'

'Where?' Richard asked. He wondered why Pinkie mentioned Laura, then realised with sinking heart that she was
no longer keeping her discontent to herself, and the echo
of it must have travelled for some distance.

'Where? Oh, a gentleman's county,' Pinkie replied,
wallowing through his barrier of ice, 'Say Northampton-
shire. You can drive up every morning easily, be in the
office by ten, down in the evening by half past six. I
calculate you could spend about 60 per cent of your
life at work and 40 per cent at home. Not too bad, that.
Mind you, these Jacobean properties don't come on the

market every day. We just happen to be more lucky at laying hands on them than most. Or Norfolk, of course, if you're interested in small boats.'

Richard wondered why living on a largish boat should automatically make him interested in small ones.

'Not Norfolk, I think.' A number of Laura's relations lived there, but he had not come to the Relais to discuss them. 'You wouldn't make a profit on *Lord Jim* anyway,' he added, 'I don't regard her as an investment.'

'Then what in the name of Christ did you buy her for?'

This was the question Richard did not want to answer. Meanwhile, the waiter put a warm plate printed with a name and device in front of each of them and, after a short interval, took it away again, this, presumably, representing the cover for which the restaurant made a charge. Subsequently he brought various inedible articles, such as bread dried to a crisp, and questionable pieces of shellfish, and placed these in front of them. Pinkie chewed away at a raw fragment.

'We might call him an old shellback, if you think that'd go down better, instead of an Ancient Mariner.'

'Who?'

'This Willis of yours. It doesn't do to be too literary.'

The waiter invited them to choose between coq au vin and navarin of lamb, either of which, in other circumstances, would have been called stew.

'Knows his job, that fellow,' said Pinkie. Richard felt inclined to agree with him.

The wine, though Richard was not the kind of person whom the sommelier kept waiting, was not particularly good. Pinkie said nothing about this because he was dazed by gin, and was not paying, and Richard said nothing because, after a little thought, he concluded that the wine was good enough for Pinkie.

After they had been given the coq au vin the waiter shovelled on to their plates, from a mysteriously divided dish, some wilted vegetables, and Richard recognised that the moment had come to make his only point.

'I really haven't any particular interest in the sale, except that I want to do the best that I can for this retired artist, Sam Willis,' he said. 'I regard him as a friend, and you remember that apart from all this local colour, I gave you the specifications of his boat.'

'Oh, I dare say. They'll have those in the office. The invaluable Miss Barker. Well, proceed.'

'There wasn't any mention, I think I'm right in saying, of a survey — that rested with the purchaser.'

Another waiter brought round a trolley on which were a number of half-eaten gateaux decorated with a white substance, and some slices of hard apple resting in water, in a glass bowl. The idea of eating these things seemed absurd, and yet Pinkie asked for some.

'Well, these specifications. I'll have to go back to the

shop, and check up on them, as I said, but I imagine you won't grudge me a glass of brandy first.'

Richard gave the order. 'There's something which I didn't mention, but I want to make it absolutely clear, and that is that I've reason to believe that this craft, the *Dreadnought*, leaks quite badly.'

Pinkie laughed, spraying a little of the brandy which had been brought to him onto the laden air. 'Of course she does. All these old boats leak like sieves. Just as all these period houses are as rotten as old cheese. Everyone knows that. But age has its value.'

Richard sighed. 'Has it ever struck you, Pinkie, what it would be like to belong to a class of objects which gets more valuable as it gets older? Houses, oak-trees, furniture, wine, I don't care what! I'm thirty-nine, I'm not sure about you . . .'

The idea was not taken up, and half an hour later Richard signed the bill and they left the Relais together. Pinkie could still think quite clearly enough to know that he had very little prospect of a new commission. 'As you're fixed, Richard,' he said, half embracing his friend, but impeded by his umbrella, 'as you're fixed, and you're an obstinate bugger, I can't shake you, you're living nowhere, you don't belong to land or water.' As Richard did not respond, he added, 'Keep in touch. We mustn't let it be so long next time.'

*   *   *

The second or third lots of clients sent along by Pinkie, an insurance broker and his wife, who wanted somewhere to give occasional parties in summer, at high tide only, were very much taken with *Dreadnought*. It was raining slightly on the day of inspection, but Willis, who had not been able to lay hands on his waterproof 'tile', but made do with a deep-crowned felt hat, stood on duty under the gap in the weather-boards, while an unsuspecting clerk from the agency showed the rest of the boat. The galley was very cramped, but the ship's chests, still marked FOR 2 SEAMEN, and the deckhouse, from which Willis had watched the life of the river go by, both made a good impression.

'You'll have noticed the quality of the bottom planking,' said the clerk. 'All these ends are 2½ English elm for three strakes out from the centre, and after that you've got oak. That's what Nelson meant, you know, when he talked about wooden walls. Mind, I don't say that she hasn't been knocked about a bit . . . There may be some weathering here and there . . .'

After a few weeks which to Willis, however, seemed like a few years, the broker's solicitors made a conditional offer for the poor old barge, and finally agreed to pay £1500, provided that *Dreadnought* was still in shipshape condition six months hence, in the spring of 1962.

Six months, Willis repeated. It was a long time to wait, but not impossible.

Richard suggested that the intervening time could well be spent in replacing the pumps and pump-wells, and certain sections of the hull. It was difficult for him to realise that he was dealing with, or rather trying to help, a man who had never, either physically or emotionally, felt the need to replace anything. Even Willis's appearance, the spiky short black hair and the prize-fighter's countenance, had not changed much since he had played truant from Elementary school and gone down to hang about the docks. If truth were known, he had had a wife, as well as a perdurable old mother, a great bicyclist and supporter of local Labour causes, but both of them had died of cancer, no replacements possible there. The body must either repair itself or stop functioning, but that is not true of the emotions, and particularly of Willis's emotions. He had come to doubt the value of all new beginnings and to put his trust in not much more than the art of hanging together. *Dreadnought* had stayed afloat for more than sixty years, and Richard, Skipper though he was, didn't understand timber. Tinkering about with the old boat would almost certainly be the end of her. He remembered the last time he had been to see the dentist. Dental care was free in the 60s, in return for signing certain unintelligible documents during the joy of escape from the surgery. But when the dentist had announced that it was urgently necessary to extract two teeth Willis had got up and walked away, glad that he hadn't taken off his coat and so would not have to enter into any further discussion while he recovered it from the waiting-room. If one goes, he thought, still worse two, they all go.

'*Dreadnought* is good for a few years yet,' he insisted. 'And what kind of repairs can you do on oak?'

'Have you asked him about the insurance valuation?' Laura asked Richard.

'There isn't one. These old barges – well, they could get a quotation for fire, I suppose, but not against flood or storm damage.'

'I'm going home for a fortnight. It may be more than a fortnight – I don't really know how long.'

'When?'

'Oh, quite soon. I'll need some money.'

Richard avoided looking at her, for fear she should think he meant anything particular by it.

'What about *Grace*?' Laura went on.

'What about her?'

'Is *Grace* in bad condition?'

Richard sighed. 'Not as good as one would like. There the trouble is largely above the waterline, though. I've told Nenna time and again that she ought to get hold of some sort of reliable chap, an ex-Naval chippie would be the right sort, just to spend the odd day on board and put everything to rights. There aren't any partitions between the cabins, to start with.'

'Did Nenna tell you that?'

'You can see for yourself, if you drop in there.'

'What a very odd thing to tell you.'

'I suppose people have got used to bringing me their queries, to some extent,' said Richard, going into their cabin to take off his black shoes and put on a pair of red leather slippers, which, like all his other clothes, never seemed to wear out. The slippers made him feel less tired.

'There are more queries from *Grace* than from *Dreadnought*, aren't there?'

'I'm not sure. I've never worked it out exactly.'

'They're not worth talking about anyway. I expect they talk about us.'

'Oh, do you think so?'

'They say "There goes that Mrs Blake again. She turns me up, she looks so bleeding bored all day".'

Richard did not like to have to think about two things at once, particularly at the end of the day. He kissed Laura, sat down, and tried to bring the two subjects put to him into order, and under one heading. A frown ran in a slanting direction between his eyebrows and halfway up his forehead. Laura's problem was that she had not enough to do — no children, though she hadn't said anything about this recently — and his heart smote him because he had undertaken to make her happy, and hadn't. Nenna, on the other hand, had rather too much. If her husband had let her down, as was apparently the case, she ought to have a male relation of some kind, to see to things. In Richard's experience, all women had plenty of male relations. Laura, for instance, had two younger brothers, who were not settling very well into the stockbrokers' firm in which they had been placed, and numerous uncles, one of them an old horror who obtained Scandinavian au pairs through advertisements in *The Lady*, and then, of course, her Norfolk cousins. Nenna appeared to have no-one. She had come over here from Canada, of course. This last reflection — it was Nova Scotia, he was pretty sure — seemed to tidy up the whole matter, which his mind now presented as a uniform interlocking structure, with working parts.

Laura was very lucky to be married to Richard, who would not have hurt her feelings deliberately for the whole world. A fortnight with her parents, he was thinking now, on their many acres of damp earth, must surely bring home to her the advantages of living on *Lord Jim*. Of course, it hadn't so far done anything of the kind, and he had to arrive at the best thing to do in the circumstances. He was not quite satisfied with the way his mind was working. Something was out of phase. He did not recognise it as hope.

'I want to take you out to dinner, Lollie,' he said.

'Why?'

'You look so pretty, I want other people to see you.

I daresay they'll wonder why on earth you agreed to go out with a chap like me.'

'Where do you go when you take people out to lunch from the office?'

'Oh, the Relais, but that's no good in the evening. We could try that Provençal place. Give them a treat.'

'You don't really want to go,' said Laura, but she disappeared into the spare cabin, where, unfortunately, her dresses had to be kept. Richard took off his slippers and put on his black shoes again, and they went out.

6

MARTHA and Tilda were in the position of having no spending money, but this was less important when they were not attending school and were spared the pains of comparison, and they felt no bitterness against their mother, because she hadn't any either. Nenna believed, however, that she would have some in the spring, when three things would happen, each, like melting ice-floes, slowly moving the next one on. Edward would come and live on *Grace*, which would save the rent he was paying on his rooms at present; the girls, once they were not being prayed for at the grotto, would agree to go back to the nuns; and with Tilda at school she could go out herself and look for a job.

Martha could not imagine her mother going out to work and felt that the experiment was likely to prove disastrous.

'You girls don't know my life,' said Nenna, 'I worked in my vacations before the war, wiping dishes, camp counselling, all manner of things.'

Martha smiled at the idea of these dear dead days. 'What did you counsel?' she asked.

The girls needed money principally to buy singles by Elvis Presley and Cliff Richard, whose brightly smiling photograph presided over their cabin. They had got the photograph as a fold-in from *Disc Weekly*. If you couldn't afford the original records, there were smaller ones you could buy at the Woolworths in the King's Road, which sounded quite like.

Like the rest of London's river children, they knew that the mud was a source of wealth, but were too shrewd to go into competition with the locals from Partisan Street for coins, medals and lugworms. The lugworms, in any case, Willis had told them, were better on Limehouse Reach. Round about *Grace* herself, the great river deposited little but mounds of plastic containers.

Every expedition meant crossing the Bridge, because the current on Battersea Reach, between the two bridges, sets towards the Surrey side. The responsibility for these outings, which might or might not be successful, had worn between Martha's eyebrows a faint frown, not quite vertical, which exactly resembled Richard's.

'We'll go bricking to-day,' she said. 'How's the tide?'

'High water Gravesend 3 a.m., London Bridge 4, Battersea Bridge 4.30,' Tilda chanted rapidly. 'Spring tide, seven and a half hour's ebb, low tide at 12.'

Martha surveyed her sister doubtfully. With so much specialised knowledge, which would qualify her for nothing much except a pilot's certificate, with her wellingtons over which the mud of many tides had dried, she had the air of something aquatic, a demon from the depths, perhaps. Whatever happens, I must never leave her behind, Martha prayed.

Both the girls were small and looked exceptionally so as they crossed the Bridge with their handcart. They wore stout Canadian anoraks, sent them by their Aunt Louise.

Below the old church at Battersea the retreating flood had left exposed a wide shelf of mud and gravel. At intervals the dark driftwood lay piled. Near the draw dock some longshoremen had heaped it up and set light to it, to clear the area. Now the thick blue smoke gave out a villainous smell, the gross spirit of salt and fire. Tilda loved that smell, and stretched her nostrils wide.

Beyond the dock, an old wrecked barge lay upside down. It was shocking, even terrifying, to see her dark flat shining bottom, chine uppermost. A derelict ship turns over on her keel and lies gracefully at rest, but there is only one way up for a Thames barge if she is to maintain her dignity.

This wreck was the *Small Gains*, which had gone down more than twenty-five years before, when hundreds of barges were still working under sail. Held fast in the mud with her cargo of bricks, she had failed to come up with the rising tide and the water had turned her over. The old bricks were still scattered over the foreshore. After a storm they were washed back in dozens, but most of them were broken or half ground to powder. Along with the main cargo, however, *Small Gains* had shipped a quantity of tiles. At a certain moment in the afternoon the sun, striking across the water from behind the gas works, sent almost level rays over the glistening Reach. Then it was possible for the expert to pick out a glazed tile, though only if it had sunk at the correct angle to the river bed.

'Do you think Ma's mind is weakening?' Tilda asked.

'I thought we weren't going to discuss our affairs today.' Martha relented and added – 'Well, Ma is much too dependent on Maurice, or on anyone sympathetic. She ought to avoid these people.'

The two girls sat on the wall of Old Battersea church-yard to eat their sandwiches. These contained a substance called Spread, and, indeed, that was all you could do with it.

'Mattie, who would you choose, if you were compelled at gunpoint to marry tomorrow?'

'You mean, someone off the boats?'

'We don't know anybody else.'

Seagulls, able to detect the appearance of a piece of bread at a hundred yards away, advanced slowly towards them over the shelving ground.

'I thought perhaps you meant Cliff.'

'Not Cliff, not Elvis. And not Richard, he's too obvious.'

Martha licked her fingers.

'He looks tired all the time now. I saw him taking Laura out to dinner yesterday evening. Straight away after he'd come back from work! Where's the relaxation in that? What sort of life is that for a man to lead?'

'What was she wearing?'

'I couldn't make out. She had her new coat on.'

'But you saw the strain on his features?'

'Oh, yes.'

'Do you think Ma notices?'

'Oh, everybody does.'

When the light seemed about right, striking fire out of the broken bits of china and glass, they went to work. Tilda lay down full length on a baulk of timber. It was her job to do this, because Martha bruised so easily. A princess, unknown to all about her, she awaited the moment when these bruises would reveal her true heritage.

Tilda stared fixedly. It was necessary to get your eye in.

'There's one!'

She bounded off, as though over stepping stones, from one object to another that would scarcely hold, old tyres, old boots, the ribs of crates from which the seagulls were dislodged in resentment. Far beyond the point at which the mud became treacherous and from which *Small Gains* had never risen again, she stood poised on the handlebars of a sunken bicycle. How had the bicycle ever got there?

'Mattie, it's a Raleigh!'

'If you've seen a tile, pick it up straight away and come back.'

'I've seen two!'

With a tile in each hand, balancing like a circus performer, Tilda returned. Under the garish lights of the Big Top, every man, woman and child rose to applaud. Who, they asked each other, was this newcomer, who had succeeded where so many others had failed?

The nearest clean water was from the standpipe in the churchyard; they did not like to wash their finds there, because the water was for the flowers on the graves, but Martha fetched some in a bucket.

As the mud cleared away from the face of the first tile, patches of ruby-red lustre, with the rich glow of a jewel's heart, appeared inch by inch, then the outlines of a delicate grotesque silver bird, standing on one leg in a circle of blue-black leaves and berries, its beak of burnished copper.

'Is it beautiful?'

'Yes.'

'And the dragon?'

The sinuous tail of a dragon, also in gold and jewel colours, wreathed itself like a border round the edge of the other tile.

The reverse of both tiles was damaged, and on only one of them the letters NDS END could just be made out, but Martha could not be mistaken.

'They're de Morgans, Tilda. Two of them at one go, two of them in one morning.'

'How much can we sell them for?'

'Do you remember the old lady, Tilda?'

'Did I see her?'

'Tilda, I only took you three months ago. Mrs Stirling, I mean, in Battersea Old House. Her sister was married to William de Morgan, that had the pottery, and made these kind of tiles, that was in Victorian days, you must remember. She was in a wheelchair. We paid for tea, but the money went to the Red Cross. We were only supposed to have two scones each, otherwise the Red Cross couldn't expect to make a profit. She explained, and she showed us all those tiles and bowls, and the brush and comb he used to do his beard with.'

'How old was she?'

'In 1965 she'll be a hundred.'

'What was her name?'

'Mrs Wilhemina Stirling.'

Tilda stared at the brilliant golden-beaked bird, about which there was something frightening.

'We'd better wrap it up. Someone might want to steal it.'

Sobered, like many seekers and finders, by the presence of the treasure itself, they wrapped the tiles in Tilda's anorak, which immediately dimmed their lustre once again with a film of mud.

'There's Woodie!'

Tilda began to jump up and down, like a cork on the tide.

'What's he doing?'

'He's getting his car out.'

There were no garages near the boats and Woodie was obliged to keep his immaculate Austin Cambridge in the yard of a public house on the Surrey side.

'I'm attracting his attention,' Tilda shouted. 'He can drive us home, and we can put the pushcart on the back seat.'

'Tilda, you don't understand. He'd have to say yes, because he's sorry for us, I heard him tell Richard we were no better than waifs of the storm, and we should ruin the upholstery, and be taking advantage of his kindness.'

'It's his own fault if he's kind. It's not the kind who inherit the earth, it's the poor, the humble, and the meek.'

'What do you think happens to the kind, then?'

'They get kicked in the teeth.'

Woodie drove them back across the bridge.

'You'll have to look after yourselves this winter, you know,' he said. 'No more lifts, I'm afraid, I shall be packed up and gone till spring. I'm thinking of laying up *Rochester* in dry dock. She needs a bit of attention.'

'Do you have to manage all that packing by yourself?' Tilda asked.

'No, dear, my wife's coming to give me a hand.'

'You haven't got a wife!'

'You've never seen her, dear.'

'What's her name?'

'Janet.' Woodie began to feel on the defensive, as though he had made the name up.

'What does she look like?'

'She doesn't much care for the river. She spends the summer elsewhere.'

'Has she left you, then?'

'Certainly not. She's got a caravan in Wales, a very nice part, near Tenby.' Although Woodie had given this explanation pretty often, he was surprised to have to make it to a child of six. 'Then in the winter we go back to our house in Purley. It's an amicable arrangement.'

Was there not, on the whole of Battersea Reach, a couple, married or unmarried, living together in the ordinary way? Certainly, among the fairweather people on the middle Reach. They lived together and even multiplied, though the opportunity for a doctor to hurry over the gangplank with a black bag, and, in his turn, fall into the river, had been missed. *Bluebird*, which was rented by a group of nurses from the Waterloo Hospital, had been at the ready, and when the birth was imminent they'd seen to it that the ambulance arrived promptly. But, apart from *Bluebird*, the middle Reach would be empty by next week, or perhaps the one after.

Martha, who had decided to stop thinking about the inconvenience they were causing, asked Woodie not to stop at the boats; they would like to go on to the New King's Road.

'We want to stop at the Bourgeois Gentilhomme,' she said, with the remnants of the French accent the nuns had carefully taught her.

'Isn't that an antique shop, dear?'

'Yes, we're going to sell an antique.'

'Have you got one?'

'We've got two.'

'Are you sure you've been to this place before?'

'Yes.'

'I shall have to pull up as near as I can and let you out,' said Woodie. He wondered if he ought to wait, but he wanted to get back to *Rochester* before she came afloat. He watched the two girls, who, to do them justice, thanked him very nicely, they weren't so badly brought up when you came to think about it, approach the shop by the side door.

On occasions, Martha's courage failed her. The advantages her sister had in being so much younger presented themselves forcibly. She sharply told Tilda, who had planted herself in a rocking-chair put out on the pavement, that she must come into the shop and help her speak to the man. Tilda, who had never sat in a rocker before, replied that her boots were too dirty.

'And anyway, I'm old Abraham Lincoln, jest sittin and thinkin.'

'You've got to come.'

The Bourgeois Gentilhomme was one of many enterprises in Chelsea which survived entirely by selling antiques to each other. The atmosphere, once through the little shop-door, cut down from a Victorian billiard-table, was oppressive. Clocks struck widely different hours. At a corner table, with her back turned towards them, sat a woman in black, apparently doing some accounts, and surrounded by dusty furniture; perhaps she had been cruelly deserted on her wedding day, and had sat there ever since, refusing to have anything touched. She did not look up when the girls came in, although the billiard table was connected by a cord to a cow-bell, which jangled harshly.

'Where's Mr Stephen, please?'

Without waiting for or expecting a reply, Martha and the reluctant Tilda walked through into the back office. Here no conversion had been done to the wretched little room, once a scullery, with two steps down to a small yard stacked high with rubbish. Mr Stephen, sitting by a paraffin heater, was also writing on pieces of paper, and appearing to be adding things up. Martha took out the two tiles and laid them in front of him.

Well used to the treasures of the foreshore, the dealer wiped the gleaming surfaces free, not with water this time, but with something out of a bottle. Then, after carefully taking off his heavy rings, he picked each of the tiles up in turn, holding them up by the extreme edge.

'So you brought these all this long way to show me. What did you think they were?'

'I know what they are. I only want to know how much you can pay me for them.'

'Have you any more of these at home?'

'They weren't at home.'

'Where did you find them, then?'

'About the place.'

'And you're sure there aren't any more?'

'Just the two.'

Mr Stephen examined the gold and silver bird through a glass.

'They're quite pretty tiles, dear, not anything more than that.'

'Then why did you take your rings off so carefully?'

'I'm always careful, dear.'

'These are ruby lustre tiles by William de Morgan,' said Martha, 'with decoration in gold and silver – the "starlight and moonlight" lustre.'

'Who sent you in here?' Mr Stephen asked.

'Nobody, you know us, we've been in before.'

'Yes, but I mean, who told you what to say?'

'Nobody.'

'Mrs Wilhemina Stirling,' Tilda put in, 'ninety-seven if she's a day.'

'Well, whoever you're selling for, I'm sorry to disappoint you, but these tiles can't be by de Morgan. I'm afraid you just don't know enough about it. I don't suppose you looked at what's left of the lettering on the reverse. NDS END. William de Morgan had his potteries in Cheyne Walk, and later he moved his kilns to Merton Abbey. This is not the mark for either one of those.'

'Of course it isn't. These are part of a very late set. His very last pottery was at Sands End, in Fulham. Didn't you know that?'

Dignity demanded that the dealer should hand the tiles back with a pitying smile. But he could not resist holding the bird up to his desk lamp, so that the light ran across the surface and seemed to flow over the edges in crimson flame. And now Martha and he were united in a strange fellow feeling, which neither of them had expected, and which they had to shake off with difficulty.

'Well, I think perhaps we can take these. The bird is much the finer of the two, of course – I'm only taking the dragon to make a pair with the bird. Perhaps you'd like to exchange them for something else in my shop. There are some charming things out there in front – some very old toys. Your little sister here . . .'

'I hate very old toys,' Tilda said. 'They may have been all right for very old children.'

'A Victorian musical box . . .'

'It's broken.'

'I think not,' said the dealer, leaving the girls and hastening out front. He began to search irritably for the key. The woman sitting at the table made no attempt to help him.

'Tilda, have you been tinkering about with the musical box?'

'Yes.'

Martha saw that discovery, which could not be long delayed, would reduce her advantage considerably.

'We're asking three pounds for the two De Morgan lustre tiles. Otherwise I must trouble you to hand them back at once.'

Tilda's respect for her sister, whom she had never seen before in the possession of so much money, reduced her almost to silence; in a hoarse whisper she asked whether they were going to get the records straight away.

'Yes, we will, but we ought to get a present for Ma first. You know Daddy always used to forget to give her anything.'

'Did she say so?'

'Have you ever actually seen anything that he's given her?'

They walked together down the King's Road, went into Woolworths, and were dazzled.

7

THE same flood tide that had brought such a good harvest of tiles heaped a mass of driftwood onto the Reach. Woodie looked at it apprehensively. He wouldn't, of course, as he usually did, have to spend the months in Purley worrying about *Rochester*, and wondering whether she was getting knocked about by flotsam in his absence. There were only a few weeks now before she went into dry dock. Perhaps he half realised that the absence of worry would make his winter unendurable. As though clinging to the last moments of a vanishing pleasure, he counted the baulks of timber edging darkly towards the boats.

His wife had already arrived from Wales. He had in prospect a time of truce, while Janet, an expert manager, in a trouser suit well adapted to the task, gave him very real help with the laying-up, but at the same time made a series of unacceptable comparisons between the caravan and *Rochester*. These comparisons were never made or implied once they were both back in Purley. They arose only in the short uneasy period passed between land and water.

As he crossed *Grace*'s deck Woodie looked up with

astonishment at *Dreadnought*, which was a bigger boat, and, having much less furniture on board, rode higher in the water. In the lighted deckhouse he could not only see old Willis, fiddling about with what looked like tins and glasses, but Janet, wearing her other trouser suit.

'It's a celebration,' said Nenna, coming up to the hatch, 'they're only waiting for you to come. It's because Willis has sold *Dreadnought*.'

'A provisional offer, I should call it. Still, it's not my object to spoil things. Aren't you going to come?'

'No, it's our turn tomorrow. The deckhouse only holds four.' And Woodie could see now that Maurice was in there as well. He never quite knew what to make of Maurice. Mrs James seemed to talk to him by the hour, in the middle of the night, sometimes, he believed, and so did the children. 'I left your two at an antique shop in the King's Road,' he said. 'They seemed to know exactly what they wanted.'

Nenna put on her jacket. She knew the Bourgeois Gentilhomme, and always feared that one day Martha might get into difficulties. If they weren't there, they were pretty sure to be in Woolworths. She started out to meet them.

Willis had noticed Woodie's return, and could be seen gesturing behind the window of the deckhouse, expressing joy, pointing him out to Janet, and waving to him to come on in.

Woodie was not feeling very sociable, as he had had, of course, to return his car to the Surrey side and walk home across the Bridge. But the deckhouse was certainly cosy, and the door, as he pulled it to behind him, cut out, to a considerable extent, the voices of the river. It was the only door on *Dreadnought* which could be considered in good repair. Even the daylong scream of the gulls was silent in here, and the hooters and sound signals arrived only as a distant complaint. For Willis, indeed, it was rather too quiet, but useful this evening when he had guests. 'We want to be able to make ourselves heard,' he said. Evidently he had toasts in mind.

In preparation, he had opened several bottles of Guinness, and one of the cans, which contained Long Life — the lady's drink — in compliment to Mrs Woodie. But he was distressed that he had no glasses.

'I shouldn't let Janet have a glass anyway,' cried Maurice, never at a loss. He explained that the lager was manufactured by the Danes, an ancient seafaring people, to be drunk straight out of the can, so that the bubbles would move straight up and down in the stomach to counteract the sideways rocking movement of the boat. To Woodie's surprise his wife laughed as though she couldn't stop. 'You never told me it was so social on the boats,' she said. He tried hard to get into the spirit of the thing. Why should a boat be less social than a caravan, for heaven's sake? He'd never seen Janet drinking out of a can before, either. But he mustn't forget that it was a great occasion for old Willis, who must be getting on for sixty-five, ready to take the knock any day now.

'It's good of you to come at such short notice, very good,' said Willis. 'I'd like to call you all shipmates. Is that passed unanimously? And now I'd like to ask how many of you go regularly to the fish-shop on Lyons Dock?'

At this moment the electricity failed, no surprise on *Dreadnought* where the wiring was decidedly makeshift. They were all in the dark, only the river lights, fixed or passing, wavered over cans, bottles and faces.

'A bit unfortunate,' said Woodie.

'Forty years ago we wouldn't have said that!' Willis exclaimed, 'Not with the right sort of woman in the room! We'd have known what to do!'

Once again Janet and Maurice laughed uproariously. The place was becoming Liberty Hall. Woodie put his hand at once, as he invariably could, on his set of pocket screwdrivers, but before he felt that it was quite tactful to offer help, Willis had lit an Aladdin, which presumably he always kept ready, no wonder. Fixed in gimbals, the lamp gradually extended its radiant circle into every corner of the deckhouse.

Maurice sprang to his feet, slightly bending his head, so as to avoid stunning himself on the roof. Although the four of them were practically knee to knee, he made as if speaking in a vast auditorium. 'Can everybody see me clearly? . . . you at the back, madam? . . . can I take it, then, that I'm heard in all parts of the house?'

Willis opened more bottles. His spectacles shone, even his leathery cheeks shone.

'Now, I was saying something about the fish-shop on Lyons Dock. If you don't ever go there, you won't have had the chance of sampling their hot mussels. They boil them in an iron saucepan. Must be iron.'

'The river's oldest delicacy!' Maurice cried.

'Oh no, they're quite fresh. I've got some boiling down below. They should be just about done now.'

'Surely mussels aren't in season?' Woodie asked.

'You're thinking of whitebait, there's no season for mussels.'

'I'm under doctor's orders, to some extent.'

'First time I've heard of it,' Janet cried.

'Mussels are at their best in autumn,' said Maurice, 'that's what they continually say in Southport.'

Encouraged, Willis offered to fetch the mussels at once, and some plates and forks and vinegar, and switch on the radio while he was gone, to give them a bit of music. Woodie was surprised to learn that there were any plates on *Dreadnought*. 'May I have the first dance, Janet?' Maurice asked, up on his feet again. Couldn't he see that there was hardly room to sit?

As Willis went to the afterhatch it struck him that *Dreadnought* was rather low in the water, almost on a level with *Grace*. He looked across to see if he could catch a glimpse of Nenna and the girls, and ask them what they thought about it, but everybody seemed to have gone ashore.

The hold was very dark, but not quite as dark as Willis had expected. In fact, it was not as dark as it should be. There were gleams and reflections where none could possibly be. Half way down the companion he stopped, and it was as though the whole length of the hold moved towards him in a body. He heard the faintest splash, and was not sure whether it was inside or out.

'What's wrong?' he thought.

Then he caught the unmistakable dead man's stench of river water, heaving slowly, but always finding, no matter what the obstacle, the shortest way home.

How bad was it?

Another step down, and the water was slopping round his ankles. His shoes filled. He bent down and put a hand in the water, and swore when an electric shock ran through his elbow and shoulder. Now he knew why the lights were out. A pale blue light puzzled him for a moment, until he realised that it was the Calor gas stove in the galley. He could just make out the bottom of the iron saucepan in which the mussels were still boiling for his guests.

The main leak had given way at last. And Willis had it in his heart to be sorry for old *Dreadnought*, as she struggled to rise against the increasing load of water. It was like one of those terrible sights of the racecourse or the battle field where wallowing living beings persevere dumbly in their duty although mutilated beyond repair.

There was a box of matches in his top pocket, but when he got them out his hands were so wet that he could not make them strike. The only hope now was to reach the hand-pump in the galley and see if he could keep the level within bounds. About a foot below the outwale there was a pretty bad hole which he'd never felt concerned him, it was so far above the waterline. He could see the shore lights through it now. If *Dreadnought* went on sinking at the present rate, in ten minutes the hole wouldn't be above the waterline, but below.

Willis set out to wade through the rolling wash. Something made for him in the darkness and struck him a violent blow just under the knee. Half believing that his leg was broken, he stooped and tried to fend the object off with his hands. It came at him again, and he could just make out that it was part of his bunk, one of the side panels. That, for some reason, almost made him give up, not the pain, but the familiar bit of furniture, the bed he had slept in for fifteen years, now hopelessly astray and as it seemed attacking him. Everything that should have stood by him had become hostile. The case of ice that weighed him down was his best suit.

He lost his footing and went right under. Totally

blinded, his spectacles streaming with water as he bobbed up, he tried to float himself into the galley. Then he realised that there was no chance of finding the hand-pump. The flood was up to the top of the stove already, and as the gas went out the saucepan went afloat and he was scalded by a stream of boiling water that mixed with the cold. There was no hope for *Dreadnought*. He would be lucky to get back up the companion.

Above in the deck-cabin the guests, for a while, noticed nothing, the music was so loud, and Maurice was so entertaining. It was said by his acquaintances in the pub that he gave value for money, but there was a touch of genius in the way he talked that night. With a keener sense of danger than the others, and finding it exhilarating, as they certainly would not, he had noticed at once that something was wrong, even before he had rubbed a clear patch on the steamy windows and, looking out into the night, had seen the horizon slowly rising, inch by inch. He made a rapid calculation. Give it a bit longer, we're all enjoying ourselves, he thought. Maurice had never learned to swim, but this did not disturb him. If only there was a piano, I could give them 'Rock of Ages' when the time comes, he said to himself.

Woodie's complaints had died down somewhat. 'Don't know about these shellfish. Taking his time about it, isn't he?'

'Never mind!' Maurice cried. 'It'll give me time to tell

both your fortunes. I just glanced at both your hands earlier on, just glanced, you know, and I seemed to see something quite unexpected written there. Now, you won't mind extending your palm, will you, Janet? You don't mind being first?'

'Do you really know how to do it?'

Maurice smiled radiantly.

'I do it almost every night. You'd be surprised how many new friends I make in that way.'

'I've got a copper bracelet on, that I wear for rheumatism,' she said, 'will that affect your reading?'

'Believe me, it won't make the slightest difference,' said Maurice.

The door opened, and Willis stood there, like a drowned man risen from the dead, his spectacles gone, water streaming from him and instantly making a pool at his feet. *Dreadnought*'s deck was still a foot or so above the tide. He was able to escort his guests, in good order, across *Grace* for Maurice, while the Woodies retreated over the gangplank to *Rochester*.

It is said on the river that a Thames barge, once she has risen with the tide, never sinks completely. But *Dreadnought*, let alone all her other weak places, had been holed amidships by a baulk of timber, and before long the water poured into her with a sound like a sigh and she went down in a few seconds.

*   *   *

The loss of *Dreadnought* meant yet another meeting of the boat-owners on *Lord Jim*, more relaxed in atmosphere than the former one, because it seemed that Mrs Blake was away, but hushed by the nature of Willis's misfortune. And yet this too had its agreeable counterpart; their boats, however much in need of repair, had not gone down.

One glass of brown sherry each – the best, there was no second best on *Lord Jim* – restored the impression of a funeral. Richard consulted a list. He wrote lists on special blank pages at the end of his diary, and tore them out only when they were needed, so that they were never lost. With care, there was no need to lose anything, particularly, perhaps, a boat. The disaster having taken place, however, the meeting must concern itself only with practical remedies.

Grace had already taken in all that could be salvaged of Willis's clothing, for drying and mending. The nuns, Nenna's nuns, what a very long time ago it seemed, in a class known as plain sewing, had taught her bygone arts, darning, patching, reinforcing collars with tape, which at last found their proper object in Willis's outmoded garments. Richard congratulated *Grace*. Nenna thought: I'm pleased for him to see that I can make a proper job of something. Why am I pleased?

Far greater sacrifices were required from *Rochester*, who volunteered to take Willis in as a lodger. At a reasonable rent, Richard suggested – but the Woodies wanted no payment. It would, after all, only be for a week or so, after that they were due back at Purley.

'That seems satisfactory, then – he can go straight to you after he comes out of hospital,' – Willis had been admitted to the Waterloo, where it was exceedingly difficult to get a bed, once more with the help of the nurses on *Bluebird*.

'And now, if you'll excuse me, I'm going on to the worst problem of the lot – Willis's financial position . . . Not the sort of thing any of us would usually discuss in public, but essential, I'm afraid, in the present case. I've been on to the PLA and they confirm that *Dreadnought* has been officially classed as a wreck, and what's worse, I'm afraid, is that she's lying near enough to the shipping channels for them, to quote their letter, to exercise their statutory powers and remove her by means of salvage craft.'

'Will that matter?' Woodie asked. 'She'll never be raised again,' and Maurice suggested that Willis would be much better off if he didn't have to look at the wreck of *Dreadnought* at every low tide.

'I quite accept that, but, to continue, all expenses of salvage and towage will be recoverable from the owners of the craft. I'm not too sure, to be quite honest with you, that Willis will be able to pay any, let alone all, of these expenses. I can't see any way out but a subscription list, to be organised as soon as possible. If there are any other suggestions . . .'

There were none, and it being obvious who would have to head the subscribers, Richard wound up the meeting by reading aloud a letter from Willis, delivered by way of *Bluebird*, in which, addressing them all as shipmates, he sent them all a squeeze of the hand and God bless. The words sounded strange in Richard's level unassuming voice, which, however quiet, always commanded attention. The catastrophe had evidently relaxed Willis's habitual control, and he had spoken from the heart, but who could tell how much else survived?

Three days later, Richard came along to *Grace* early in the morning, and told her that there was a call for her. The only telephone on the Reach was on *Lord Jim*. If this was inconvenient, Richard did not say so, although to be called to the telephone, or wanted on the telephone, as Richard put it, always seemed a kind of reproach in itself. More awkward still, since Laura was not on board, he was obliged to lock up before going to the office, and had to wait on board, with his brief-case and umbrella, determinedly not listening, while Nenna went down to the saloon.

Nenna felt sure that there was no-one that it could be but Edward. Although it was very unlikely, he must have got the number from the boat company.

'Hullo, Nenna! This is Louise! Yes it's Louise!'

'Louise!'

'Didn't you get my last letter?'

'I don't think so. They get lost sometimes.'

'How come?'

'People fetch them from the office and mean to take them round, and then they get lost or dropped in the water.'

'That's absolutely absurd, Nenna dear.'

'What does it matter anyway? Where are you, Louise, can I come right over and see you?'

'Not right now, Nenna.'

'Where are you calling from?'

'From Frankfurt on the Rhine. We're over here on a business trip. Too bad you didn't read my letters. Has Heinrich arrived?'

'God, Louise, who is Heinrich?'

'Nenna, I know all your intonations as well as I know my own, and I can tell that you're in a very bad state. Joel and I have a suggestion about that which we're going to put to you as soon as we get to London.'

'I'm quite all right, Louise. You're coming here, then?'

'And Edward. Exactly what is the position in regard to your marriage? Is Edward still with you?'

Nenna was a child again. She felt her responsibilities slipping away one by one, even her marriage was going.

'Oh, Louise, do you still have lobster sandwiches at Harris's?'

'Now, this boat of yours. What number is this I'm calling you on, by the way? Is that the yacht club?'

'Not exactly . . . it's a friend.'

'Well, this boat you and the children are living on. I understand very well how people live year round in houseboats on the Seine, but not on the Thames, isn't it tidal?'

'Why, yes, it is.'

'And this boat of yours — is she crewed, or is it a bareboat rental?'

'Neither really. I've bought her.'

'Where do you sail her then?'

'She never sails, she's at moorings.'

'We were reading in the London *Times* that some kind of boat was sunk on the Thames the other day. In one of the small paragraphs. Joel reads it all through. He says it's so long since he saw you and the girls that he won't know you. In any case, as I said, we have certain plans which we'd like to put before you, and in the meantime I want you to say hello from us to young Heinrich.'

'Louise, don't ring off. Whatever it's costing. I've never met young Heinrich.'

'Well, neither have we, of course. Didn't you get my letter?'

'It seems not, Louise.'

'He's the son of a very good business friend of ours, who's sent him to school at Sales Abbey, that's with the

Benedictines, and he's currently returning home, he has permission to leave school early this term for some reason and return home.'

'Does he live in Frankfurt on the Maine?'

'On the Rhine. No, not at all, he's Austrian, he lives in Vienna. He just requires to spend one night in London, he's due to catch a flight to Vienna the next day.'

'Do you mean that he expects to come and stay on *Grace*?'

'Who is Grace, Nenna?'

'What's the name of this boy?' Nenna asked.

'His parents are a Count and Countess, in business as I told you, of course all that doesn't mean anything now, but they're in very good standing. He should have been with you last Friday.'

'Well, he wasn't. There must have been a misunderstanding about that ... Oh, Lou, you don't know how good it is to hear your voice ...'

'Nenna, you're becoming emotional. Wouldn't you agree it's just about time that somebody helped you to restore some kind of order into your life?'

'Oh, please don't do that!'

'I hate to cut you short,' said Richard from the hatch, 'it's only that I can hardly expect my staff to be in time if I'm late myself.'

His voice was courteous to the point of diffidence, and Nenna, giving way a little, let herself imagine what it

would be like to be on Richard's staff, and to be directed
in everything else by Louise, and to ebb and flow without
volition, in the warmth of love and politeness.

'Goodbye, Louise. As soon as you get to England. –
Forgive me, Richard, it was my sister, I don't know how
she got your number, I haven't seen her in five years.'

'I sensed that she wasn't used to being contradicted.'

'No.'

'She was very firm.'

'That's so.'

'Are you sure she's your sister?'

'As far as he's concerned, I'm just a drifter,' Nenna
thought, smiling and thanking him. Richard patted himself to see that he had some matches on him, a gesture
which appealed to Nenna, and walked off up the Embankment to call a taxi.

I won't go down without a struggle, Nenna thought. I
married Edward because I wanted to live with him, and
I still do. While she ironed Willis's stiff underclothes
which, aired day after day, never seemed to get quite
dry, the accusations against her, not inside her mind
but at some point detached from it, continued without
pause. They were all the more tedious because they were
reduced, for all practical purposes, to one question: why,
after everything that has been put forward in this court,
have you still made no attempt to visit 42b Milvain Street?

Nenna wished to reply that it was not for the expected reasons – not pride, not resentment, not even the curious acquired characteristics of the river dwellers, which made them scarcely at home in London's streets. No, it's because it's my last chance. While I've still got it I can take it out and look at it and know I still have it. If that goes, I've nothing left to try.

She told Martha that she would be going out that evening and would quite likely not be back until the following day.

'Well, where do we stay?'

'On *Rochester*. I'll ask them.'

In less than a week the impeccable *Rochester* had been transformed into a kind of boarding-house. Nenna would never have dreamed before this of asking them to look after the girls. Willis, on his return from hospital, had taken up his quarters there, though he was no trouble, remaining quietly in the spare cabin without even attempting to watch the river's daily traffic. He had not come up on deck when the PLA tug arrived, and the poor wreck had been towed away, still under water, but surfacing from time to time as though she had still not quite admitted defeat.

'That's just a launch tug,' said Tilda, 'under forty tons. It didn't take much to move *Dreadnought*.'

The salvage men returned what they could, including the iron saucepan, but Willis's painting materials were past repair. Nothing was said about his next move, except that he could hardly expect his sister to take him in now, and that he was unwilling, under any circumstances, to move to Purley. Therefore the daily life of the Woodies, which had depended almost entirely on knowing what they would be doing on any given day six months hence, fell into disrepair. They had to resort to unpacking many of the things which they had so carefully stowed away. They repeated, however, that Willis was no trouble.

When Nenna told them that she had urgent business on the other side of London and that she would have to ask whether Martha and Tilda could stay the night, *Rochester* accepted without protest, and they went over, taking with them their nightdresses, Cliff records, the Cliff photograph and two packets of breakfast cereals, for they did not like the same kind. Tilda, who had been vexed at missing the actual shipwreck, went straight down to Willis's cabin to ask him if he would draw her a picture of it. Martha confronted her mother.

'You're going to see Daddy, aren't you?'

'I might be bringing him back with me. Would you like that?'

'I don't know.'

8

BETTER take a cheap all-day ticket, the bus conductor advised, if Nenna really wanted to get from Chelsea to Stoke Newington.

'Or move house,' he advised.

Although as she changed from bus to bus she was free at last of the accusing voices, she had time for a number of second thoughts, wishing in particular that she had put on other clothes, and had had her hair cut. She didn't know if she wanted to look different or the same. Her best coat would perhaps have been better because it would make her look as though she hadn't let herself go, but on the other hand her frightful old lumber jacket would have suggested, what was true enough, that she was worried enough not to care. But among all these doubts it had not occurred to her that if she got as far as 42b Milvain Street, and rang the bell, Edward would not open the door.

It was the b, perhaps, that was the trouble. b suggested an upstairs flat, and there was only one bell at 42. The yellowish-grey brick houses gave straight on to the street, which she had found only after turning out of another one, and then another. On some doorsteps the milk was still waiting to be taken in. She still missed the rocking of the boat.

He might be in or he might be out. There was a light on in the hall, and apparently on the second floor, though that might be a landing. Nenna struggled against an impulse to rush into the fish and chip shop at the corner, the only shop in the street, and ask them if they had ever seen somebody coming out of number 42b who looked lonely, or indeed if they had ever seen anyone coming out of it at all.

The figure turning the corner and walking heavily down the road could not under any circumstances have been Edward, but at least it relieved her from the suspicion that the street was uninhabited. When the heavily-treading man slowed down at number 42, she couldn't believe her luck. He had been out and was coming in, although the way he walked suggested that going out had not been a great success, and that not much awaited him at home.

As he stopped and took out two keys tied together, neither of them a car key, Nenna faced him boldy.

'Excuse me, I should like you to let me in.'

'May I ask who you are?'

The 'may I ask' disconcerted her.

'I'm *Grace*. I mean, I'm Nenna.'

'You don't seem very sure.'

'I am Nenna James.'

'Mrs Edward James?'

'Yes. Does Edward James live here?'

'Well, in a way.' He dangled the keys from hand to hand. 'You don't look at all how I expected.'

Nenna felt rebuked.

'How old are you?'

'I'm thirty-two.'

'I should have thought you were twenty-seven or twenty-eight at most.'

He stood ruminating. She tried not to feel impatient.

'Did Edward say what I looked like, then?'

'No.'

'What *has* he been saying?'

'As a matter of fact, I very rarely speak to him.'

Nenna looked at him more closely, trying to assess him as an ally. The cuffs of his raincoat had been neatly turned. Somebody must be doing his mending for him, as she was doing Willis's, and the idea gave her a stab of pain which she couldn't relate to her other feelings. She stared up at his broad face.

'We can't stand here all night on the pavement like this,' he said, still with the two keys in his hand.

'Then hadn't you better let me in?'

'I don't know that that would be quite the right thing to do.'

'Why not?'

'Well, you might turn out to be a nuisance to Edward.'

She mustn't irritate him.

'In what way?'

'Well, I didn't care for the way you were standing there ringing the bell. Anyway, he's out.'

'How can you tell? You're only just coming in yourself. Do you live here?'

'Well, in a way.'

He examined her more closely. 'Your hair is quite pretty.'

It had begun to rain slightly. There seemed no reason why they should not stand here for ever.

'As a matter of fact,' he said, 'I do remember you. My name is Hodge. Gordon Hodge.'

Nenna shook her head. 'I can't help that.'

'I have met you several times with Edward.'

'And was I a nuisance then?'

'This isn't my house, you see. It belongs to my mother. My mother is taking your husband in, at considerable inconvenience, as a kind of paying guest.'

'He's the lodger?'

'She only agreed to it because I used to know him at school.'

Abyss after abyss of respectability was opening beneath her. How could Edward be living in a house belonging to somebody's mother, and, above all, Gordon Hodge's mother?

'Why do you very rarely speak to him?'

'We're just living here quietly, with my mother, two quiet chaps working things out for ourselves.'

A wave of cold discouragement closed over her. The disagreement about where they were to live had come to seem the only obstacle. But perhaps Edward was altogether better without her. Perhaps he knew that. He must have heard her at the door.

'Well,' said Gordon, 'you'd better come inside, I suppose.' Once the key was in the lock, he pushed forward with both hands, one on the front door, one on Nenna's back, so that in the end she was propelled into number 42. Gordon's mother had an umbrella stand and a set of Chinese temple bells in her hall.

'Carry on up.' They passed two landings, Gordon following her with majestic tread, but faster than one might expect, since although he had lost time in hanging up his raincoat in the hall, he reached the door first, and opened it without any kind of announcement, and Edward was standing, with his back to them at first, thinner and smaller than she remembered, but then she always made the mistake when she hadn't seen him for a bit – he turned round, protesting, and it was Edward.

Who else, after all, could it have been? But in her relief Nenna forgot the quiet reasonable remarks which she had rehearsed at the bus stops, and in the buses, all the way to Stoke Newington.

'Darling, darling.'

Edward looked at her with grey eyes like Tilda's, but without much expectation from life.

'Darling, aren't you surprised?'

'Not very. I've been listening to you ringing the bell.'

'How did you know it was me?'

'Nenna. Have you come all this way, after all this time, to try to get me to live on that boat?'

Nenna had forgotten about Gordon, or rather she assumed that he must have gone away, but he had not. To her amazement, he was still planted just behind her.

'Edward, Nenna. You two seem to be having a bit of a difference of opinion. Yes, let's face it, you're in dispute. And in these matters it's often helpful to have a third party present. That's how these marriage counsellors make their money, you know.'

This must have been a joke, as he laughed, or perhaps any mention of marriage was a joke to Gordon, who walked past Nenna and settled himself between them in a small chair, actually a nursing chair, surviving from some earlier larger family home and much too low for him, so that he had to try crossing his legs in several positions. He creaked, as he settled, as a boat creaks. Had he really been at the same school as Edward? His feet were now stuck out in front of him and Nenna could read the word EXCELLA on the soles of each of his new shoes.

'Get out!'

Gordon sat quite still for a few seconds, then uncrossed his legs and went out of the room, a room in his own house, or rather his mother's. Because it was theirs, he knew how to shut the door, although it did not fit very well, without any irritating noise.

'You've always known how to get rid of my friends,' Edward muttered.

Nenna was no more able to deny this than any other woman.

'He's hateful!'

'Gordon's all right.'

'We can't talk while he's around.'

'His mother has been very good to me.'

'That's ridiculous! To be in a position where you have to say that someone's mother has been very good to you – that's ridiculous! Isn't it?'

'Yes.'

'Where did you meet these Hodges anyway? I never remember you ever talking about them.'

'I had to go somewhere,' Edward said.

They had plenty of time, and yet she felt that there was almost none.

'Eddie, I'll tell you what I came to say. Why won't you come over to us for a week, or even for a night?'

'That boat! It's not for me to come to you, it's for you to get rid of it. I'm not quarrelling with you about the money. If you don't want to sell it, why can't you rent it out?'

'I don't know that I can, right away.'

'Why, what's wrong with it?'

'She's a thought damp. It would be easier in the spring.'

'Didn't I see something in the paper about one of them sinking? I don't even know if they're safe for the children!'

'Some of them are beautiful. *Lord Jim*, for instance, inside she's really better than a house.'

'Who lives on *Lord Jim*?' Edward asked with the discernment of pure jealousy, the true lover's art which Nenna was too distraught to recognise.

'I don't know, I don't care. Well, the Blakes do. Richard and Laura Blake.'

'Have they got money?'

'I suppose so.'

'They live on a boat because they think it's smart.'

'Laura doesn't.'

'What's this Richard Blake like?'

'I don't know. He was in the Navy, I think, in the war, or the RNVR.'

'Don't you know the difference?'

'Not exactly, Eddie.'

'I bet he does.'

Things were going as badly as they could. From the room immediately beneath them, somebody began to play the piano, a Chopin nocturne, with heavy emphasis, but the piano was by no means suitable for Chopin and the sound travelled upwards as a hellish tingling of protesting strings.

'Eddie, is this the only room you've got?'

'I don't see anything wrong with it.'

She noticed now that there was a kind of cupboard in the corner which was likely to contain a washbasin, and a single bed, tucked in with a plaid rug. Surely they'd do better making love on board *Grace* than on a few yards of Mackenzie tartan?

'You can't expect us to come here?'

It must be Gordon playing downstairs. There were pauses, then he banged the keys plaintively, going over the passages he hadn't been able to get right, then suddenly he put on a record of the Chopin and played along with it, always two or three notes behind.

'Eddie, what do you want? Why are you here? Why?'

He replied reluctantly, 'My job's up here.'

'I don't even know what you do. Strang Graphics! What are they?'

They were both still standing up, facing each other, at about the same height.

'Strang is an advertising firm. It's small, that's why it's up here, where the rents are low. They hope to expand later, then they'll move. I'm not going to pretend anything about my job. It's clerical.'

Edward's references from the construction firm when he left Panama had not been very good. Nenna knew that, but she was sure it couldn't have been Edward's fault, and at the moment she couldn't be bothered with it.

'You don't have to stay there! There's plenty of jobs! Anyone can get a job anywhere!'

'I can't.'

He turned his head away, and as the light caught his face at a certain angle Nenna realised in terror that he was right and that he would never get anywhere. The terror, however, was not for herself or for the children but for Edward, who might realise that what he was saying was true. She forgot whatever she had meant to tell him, went up close and took him tenderly by both ears.

'Shut up, Eddie.'

'Nenna, I'm glad you came.'

'You are?'

'Curious, I didn't mean to say that.'

She clung to him hard, she loved him and could never leave him. They were down on the floor, and one side of her face was scorched by Gordon's mother's horrible gas-fire, in front of which there was a bowl of tepid water. He stroked her face, with its one bright red cheek, one pale.

'You look as ugly as sin.'

'Wonderful.'

There was a tapping, just audible above the piano.

'Excuse me, Mrs James, I'm Gordon's mother, I thought I'd just look in, as I haven't had the pleasure of meeting you.'

Nenna got to her feet, trying to pull down her jersey.

'I hope you don't find the gas-fire too high,' said Mrs Hodge, 'it's easily lowered. You just turn the key down there on the right-hand side.'

Not receiving any response, she added, 'And I hope the music doesn't disturb you. Gordon is something of a pianist.'

'No, he isn't,' said Nenna.

The mother's face crumpled up and withered, then corrected itself to the expression of one who is in the right. She withdrew. Nenna was ashamed, but she couldn't make amends, not now. In the morning she would beg sincerely for forgiveness, less sincerely praise Gordon as a pianist, offer to help pay to have the piano seen to.

Then she looked at Edward and saw that he was furious. 'You've only come here to hurt these people.'

'I didn't. I never knew they existed. Forgive!'

'It's not a matter of forgiveness, it's a matter of common politeness.'

They were quarrelling, but at first they were not much better at it than Gordon was at Chopin.

'I want you, Eddie, that's the one and only thing I came about. I want you every moment of the day and night and every time I try to fold up a map.'

'You're raving, Nenna.'

'Please give.'

'Give you what? You're always saying that. I don't know what meaning you attach to it.'

'Give anything.'

She didn't know why she wanted this so much, either. Not presents, not for themselves, it was the sensation of being given to, she was homesick for that.

And now the quarrel was under its own impetus, and once again a trial seemed to be in progress, with both of them as accusers, but both figuring also as investigators of the lowest description, wretched hirelings, turning over the stones to find where the filth lay buried. The squash racquets, the Pope's pronouncements, whose fault it had been their first night together, an afternoon really, but not much good in either case, the squash racquets again, the money spent on *Grace*. And the marriage that was being described was different from the one they had known, indeed bore almost no resemblance to it, and there was no-one to tell them this.

'You don't want me,' Edward repeated, 'if you did, you'd have been with me all this time. All you've ever cared about is being approved of, like a little girl at a party.'

He must have forgotten what Tilda's like, she thought, and she felt frightened. But Edward went on to tell her

that she didn't really care for the children, she only liked
to think she did, to make herself feel good.

So far neither of them had raised their voices, or only
enough to be heard above Gordon's din. But when she
made a last appeal, and told him, though feeling it
was not quite true, that Martha had asked her to
bring her father back, and then, very unwisely, referred
again to Mrs Hodge, and the house, and the single
bed, and even the temple bells, and asked him why
he didn't come to his senses and whether he didn't
think he'd be happier living with a woman, whether
she was on a boat or not, he turned on her, upset-
ting the bowl of water in front of the gas fire, and
shouted:

'You're not a woman!'

Nenna was outside in the street. In leaving the room,
swelling for the first time with tears, she had collided
awkwardly with Gordon's mother, who supposed she
could stand where she liked in her own house, and even
if Edward had called after her, she would not have been
able to hear him. She walked away down Milvain Street
as fast as it was possible for her feet to hit the ground.
The fish and chip shop was still lighted and open. She had
expected to spend that night with Edward and wake up
beside him, the left-hand side, that had become a habit and
it was a mistake, no doubt, to allow marriage to become a

matter of habit, but that didn't prove that she was not a woman.

She walked down street after street, always turning to the right, and pulled herself up among buses, and near a railway bridge. Seven Sisters Road. It was late, the station was shut. Her hands were empty. She realised now for the first time that she had left her purse behind in Edward's room. That meant that she had no money, and the all-day bus ticket was of course also in the purse.

Nenna set out to walk. A mile and a half down Green Lanes, half a mile down Nassington Green Road, one and a half miles the wrong way down Balls Pond Road, two miles down Kingsland Road, and then she was lost. As is usual in such cases her body trudged on obstinately, knowing that one foot hurt rather more than the other, but deciding not to admit this until some sort of objective was reached, while her mind, rejecting the situation in time and space, became disjointed and childish. It came to her that it was wrong to pray for anything simply because you felt you needed it personally. Prayer should be beyond self, and so Nenna repeated a Hail Mary for everyone in the world who was lost in Kingsland Road without their bus fares. She had also been taught, when in difficulty, to think of a good life to imitate. Nenna thought of Tilda, who would certainly have got on to a late night bus and ridden without paying the fare, or even have borrowed money from the conductor. Richard would never have left anything behind anywhere, or, if he had, he would have gone back for it. Louise would not have made an unsuccessful marriage in the first place, and she supposed her marriage must be unsuccessful, because Edward had told her that she was not a woman.

Nenna had no more than an animal's sense of direction and distance, but it seemed to her that the right thing to do would be to try to reach the City, then, once she got to Blackfriars, she knew where the river was, and though that would be Lambeth Reach or King's Reach, a long way downstream of the boats, still, once she had got to the river she would be on the way home. She had worked in an office in Blackfriars once, before Tilda came.

That meant turning south, and she would have to ask which way she was headed. She began to look, with a somewhat dull kind of hopefulness, for somebody friendly, not too much in a hurry, walking the opposite way, although it would be more reasonable, really, to ask somebody walking the same way. Handfuls of sleet were beginning to wander through the air. Radio shop, bicycle shop, family planning shop, funeral parlour, bicycles, radio spare parts, television hire, herbalist, family planning, a florist. The window of the florist was still lit and entirely occupied by a funeral tribute, a football goal, carried out in white chrysanthemums. The red ball had just been introduced into Soccer and there was a ball in the goal, this time in red chrysanthemums. Nenna stood looking into the window, feeling the melted hail make its way down the gap between the collar of her coat and her body. One shoe seemed to be wetter than the other and the strap was working loose, so, leaning against the ledge of the shop window, she took it off to have a look at it. This made her left foot very cold, so she twisted it round her right ankle. Someone was coming, and she felt that she couldn't bear it if he, because it was a man, said, 'Having trouble with your shoe?' For an unbalanced moment she thought it might be Gordon Hodge, pursuing her to see that she would not come back, and make a nuisance of herself to Edward.

The man stood very close to her, pretended to look in the window, advanced with a curious sideways movement and said –

'Like flowers?'

'Not at the moment.'

'Fixed up for the night?'

Nenna did not answer. She was saddened by the number of times the man must have asked this question. He smelled of loneliness. Well, they always moved off in the end, though they often stayed a while, as this one did, whistling through their teeth, like stand-up comics about to risk another joke.

He snatched the shoe out of her hand and hurled it violently away from her into the Kingsland Road.

'What you going to do now?'

Nenna shook off her other shoe and began half walking and half running as fast as she could, not looking behind her, Laburnum Street, Whiston Street, Hows Street, Pearson Street, a group at the end of Cremers Street who stood laughing, probably at her. One foot seemed to be bleeding. *I expect they think I've been drinking.*

Where the Hackney Road joins Kingsland Road a taxi drew up beside her.

'You're out late.'

'I don't know what the time is.'

'A bit late for paddling. Where are you going?'

'To the river.'

'Why?'

'Why not?'

'People jump in sometimes.'

Nenna told him, without much expecting to be believed, that she lived on Battersea Reach. The driver twisted his arm backwards to open the door.

'You'd like a lift, wouldn't you?'

'I haven't any money.'

'Who said anything about money?'

She got into the warm interior of the taxi, reeking of tobacco and ancient loves, and fell asleep at once. The taxi-man drove first to Old Street, where there was a garage open all night for the trade, and bought a tankful of petrol. Then he turned through the locked and silent City and towards the Strand, where the air first begins to feel damp, blowing up the side streets with the dawn wind off the river.

'We can go round by Arthur's in Covent Garden and get a sandwich, if you want,' he said, 'that won't break the bank.'

Then he saw that his fare was asleep. He stopped and had a cup of tea himself, and explained to the Covent Garden porters, who wanted to know what he'd got in the back, that it was the Sleeping Beauty.

The taxi drew up opposite the Battersea Bridge end of the boats. Only the driver's expression showed what he thought of the idea of living in a place like that. But it might suit some people. Carefully, as one who was used to such endings, he woke Nenna up.

'You're home, dear.'

Then he made a U turn and drove away so rapidly that she could not make out his number, only the red tail light diminishing, at more than legal speed, down the deserted Embankment. She was, therefore, never able to thank him. Although it must be three or four in the morning, there were still lights showing on *Lord Jim*. Richard was standing on the afterdeck, wearing a Naval duffle coat, Arctic issue.

'What are you doing, Nenna, where are your shoes?'

'What are you doing, Richard, standing there in your greatcoat?'

Neither of them was speaking sensibly.

'My wife's left me.'

She must have done, Nenna thought, or he wouldn't call Laura 'my wife'.

'Surely she's only gone to stay with her family. You told me so.'

Although it was very unlikely that they could be disturbing anyone they both spoke almost in whispers, and Nenna's last remark, which scarcely deserved an answer, was lost in the air, drowned by the wash of high tide.

'I haven't liked to say anything about it, but you must have noticed, that evening you stayed to have a drink with us, that my wife wasn't quite herself.'

'I thought she was,' said Nenna.

Richard was startled. 'Don't you like her?'

'I can't tell. I should have to meet her somewhere else.'

'You probably think I'm an obstinate swine to make her live here on *Lord Jim*. I couldn't really believe she wouldn't like it. I'm afraid my mind doesn't move very fast, not as fast as some people's. I wanted to get her right away from her family, they're a disrupting factor, I don't mind telling you.'

'Do they play the piano?' Nenna asked. She could no longer feel her feet, but, glancing down at them, not too obviously for fear Richard should feel that he ought to do something about them, she saw that both of them were now bleeding. A hint of some religious association disturbed her. In the convent passage the Sacred Heart looked down in reproach. And suppose she had left marks on the floor of the taxi?

'Of course I wouldn't have suggested taking her to live anywhere that was below standard. I had a very good man in to see to the heating and lighting, and the whole conversion was done professionally. But I suppose that wasn't really the point. The question really was, did being alone with me on a boat seem like a good idea or not?'

'She'll come back, Richard.'

'That won't alter the fact that she went away.'

Richard evidently felt that memory must keep to its place, otherwise how could it be measured accurately?

'Nenna, you've hurt your foot!'

Overwhelmed by not having noticed this earlier, by his failure of politeness, observation and helpfulness, all that had been taught him from boyhood up, Richard proceeded at the double onto the Embankment, to escort her on to *Lord Jim*.

'They're all right, honestly, Richard. It's only a scrape.' That was the children's word. 'Just lend me a handker-chief.'

Richard was the kind of man who has two clean handkerchiefs on him at half past three in the morning. From the hold, where everything had its proper place, he fetched a bottle of TCP and a pair of half-wellingtons.

The boots looked very much too big, but she appreciated that he wouldn't have liked to lend a pair of Laura's. Or perhaps Laura had taken all her things with her.

'Your feet are rather small, Nenna.'

Richard liked things to be the right size.

'Smaller than standard, I think.' He seated her firmly on one of the lights, and, without mistake or apology, put each of her feet into one of the clean boots. Each foot in turn felt the warmth of his hands and relaxed like an animal who trusts the vet.

'I don't know why you're wandering about here in the dark anyway. Nenna, have you been to a party?'

'Do you really think I go to parties where everyone leaves their shoes behind?'

'Well, I don't know. You lead a bit of a Bohemian existence, I mean, a lot more Bohemian than I do. I mean, I know various people in Chelsea, but they don't seem very different from anyone else.'

'I've come from a bit farther than Chelsea tonight,' Nenna said.

'Please don't think I'm being inquisitive. You mustn't think I'm trying to find out about your private affairs.'

'Richard, how old are you?'

'I was born on June 2nd 1922. That made me just seventeen when the war broke out.' Richard only estimated his age in relationship to his duties.

Nenna sat moving her feet about inside the spacious

wellingtons. It was the river's most elusive hour, when darkness lifts off darkness, and from one minute to another the shadows declare themselves as houses or as craft at anchor. There was a light wind from the north-west.

'Nenna, would you like to come out in the dinghy?'

Too tired to be surprised by anything, Nenna looked at the davits and saw that the dinghy must have been lowered away already. If everything hadn't been quite in order he wouldn't, of course, have asked her.

'We can go up under Wandsworth Bridge as far as the Fina Oil Depot and then switch off and drift down with the tide.'

'Were you going to go anyway?' asked Nenna. The question seemed of great importance to her.

'No, I was hoping someone might come along and keep me company.'

'You mean you'd left it to chance?' Nenna couldn't believe this.

'I was hoping that you might come.'

Well, thought Nenna.

They had to go down the rope side-ladder, Richard first. Her feet hurt a good deal, and she thought, though not wishing to be ungrateful, that she might have done better without the boots. However, she managed to step in amidships without rocking *Lord Jim*'s dinghy by an inch.

'Cast off, Nenna.'

She was back for a moment on Bras d'Or, casting off, coiling the painter up neatly, approved of by her father, and by Louise.

It had been a test, then, she remembered, of a day's success if the outboard started up first time. Richard's Johnson, obedient to the pressed button, came to life at once, and she saw that it had never occurred to him that it mightn't. Small boats develop emotions to a fine pitch, and she felt that she would go with him to the end of the world, if his outboard was always going to start like that. And indeed, reality seemed to have lost its accustomed hold, just as the day wavered uncertainly between night and morning.

'I've been wanting to tell you, Nenna, that I very much doubt whether you're strong enough to undertake all the work you do on *Grace*. And some of the things you do seem to me to be inefficient, and consequently rather a waste of energy. For example, I saw you on deck the other morning struggling to open the lights from the outside, but of course all your storm fastenings must be on the inside.'

'We haven't got any storm fastenings. The lights are kept down with a couple of bricks. They work perfectly well.' Now she felt furious. 'Surely you don't watch me from *Lord Jim*.'

Richard considered this carefully.

'I suppose I do.'

She had been unjust. She knew that he was good, and kept an eye on everybody, and on the whole Reach.

'I shouldn't be any happier, you know, if everything on *Grace* worked perfectly.'

He looked at her in amazement.

'What has happiness got to do with it?'

The dinghy followed the left bank, passing close to the entrance to Chelsea creek. They scanned the misty water, keeping a watch-out for driftwood which might foul up the engine.

'Do you talk a great deal to Maurice?' Richard asked.

'All day and half the night, sometimes.'

'What on earth do you talk about?'

'Sex, jealousy, friendship and music, and about the boats sometimes, the right way to prime the pump, and things like that.'

'What kind of pump have you got?'

'I don't know, but it's the same as Maurice's.'

'I could show you how to prime it any time you like.' But he was not satisfied. 'When you've finished saying all that you want to say about these things, though, do you feel that you've come to any definite conclusion?'

'No.'

'So that, in the end, you've nothing definite to show for it?'

'About jealousy and music? How could we?'

'I suppose Maurice is very musical?'

'He's got a nice voice and he can play anything by ear. I've heard him play Liszt's Campanello with teaspoons, without leaving out a single note. That wasn't music, but we had a good time ... and then, I don't know, we do talk about other things, particularly I suppose the kind of fixes we're both in.'

She stopped, aware that it wouldn't be advisable for Richard to know about Harry's visits. The crisis of conscience and duty would be too painful. Yet she would have very much liked to keep nothing back from him.

'That leads up to what I've really often wanted to ask you,' Richard went on. 'It seems to me you find it quite easy to put your feelings into words.'

'Yes.'

'And Maurice?'

'Yes.'

'I don't. I'm amazed at the amount people talk, actually. I can't for the life of me see why, if you really feel something, it's got to be talked about. In fact, I should have thought it lost something, if you follow me, if you put it into words.'

Richard looked anxious, and Nenna saw that he really thought that he was becoming difficult to understand.

'Well,' she said, 'Maurice and I are talkative by nature. We talk about whatever interests us perhaps for the same reason that Willis draws it and paints it.'

'That's not the same thing at all. I like Willis's drawings.

I've bought one or two of them, and I think they'll keep up their value pretty well.'

Beyond Battersea Bridge the light, between grey and silver, cast shadows which began to follow the lighters, slowly moving round at moorings.

At a certain point, evidently prearranged, for he didn't consult Nenna and hardly glanced at the banks, Richard put about, switched off the engine and hauled it on board. Once he had fitted in the rudder to keep the dinghy straight against the set of the tide he returned to the subject. A lifetime would not be too long, if only he could grasp it exactly.

'Let's say that matters hadn't gone quite right with you, I mean personal matters, would you be able to find words to say exactly what was wrong?'

'I'm afraid so, yes, I would.'

'That might be useful, of course.'

'Like manufacturers' instructions. In case of failure, try words.'

Richard ignored this because it didn't seem to him quite to the point. On the whole, he disliked comparisons, because they made you think about more than one thing at a time. He calculated the drift. Satisfied that it would bring them exactly down to the point he wanted on the starboard side of *Lord Jim*, he asked –

'How do you feel about your husband?'

The shock Nenna felt was as great as if he had made

a mistake with the steering. If Richard was not at home with words, still less was he at home with questions of a personal nature. He might as well capsize the dinghy and be done with it. But he waited, watching her gravely.

'Aren't you able to explain?'

'Yes, I am. I can explain very easily. I don't love him any more.'

'Is that true?'

'No.'

'You're not making yourself clear, Nenna.'

'I mean that I don't hate him any more. That must be the same thing.'

'How long have you felt like this?'

'For about three hours.'

'But surely you haven't seen him lately?'

'I have.'

'You mean tonight? What happened?'

'I insulted his friend, and also his friend's mother. He gave me his opinion about that.'

'What did your husband say?'

'He said that I wasn't a woman. That was absurd, wasn't it?'

'I should imagine so, yes. Demonstrably, yes.' He tried again. 'In any ordinary sense of the word, yes.'

'I only want the ordinary sense of the word.'

'And how would you describe the way you feel about him now?' Richard asked.

'Well, I feel unemployed. There's nothing so lonely as unemployment, even if you're on a queue with a thousand others. I don't know what I'm going to think about if I'm not going to worry about him all the time. I don't know what I'm going to do with my mind.' A formless melancholy overcame her. 'I'm not too sure what to do with my body either.'

It was a reckless indulgence in self-pity. Richard looked steadily at her.

'You know, I once told Laura that I wouldn't like to be left alone with you for any length of time.'

'Why did you?'

'I don't know. I can't remember what reason I gave. It must have been an exceptionally stupid one.'

'Richard, why do you have such a low opinion of yourself?'

'I don't think that I have. I try to make a just estimate of myself, as I do of everyone else, really. It's difficult. I've a long way to go when it comes to these explanations. But I understood perfectly well what you said about feeling unemployed.'

They were up to *Lord Jim*. With only the faintest possible graze of the fender, the dinghy drifted against her.

'Where shall I tie up?'

'You can make fast to the ladder, but give her plenty of rope, or she'll be standing on end when the tide goes down.'

Nenna knew this perfectly well, but she felt deeply at peace.

As Richard stood up in the boat, he could be seen to hesitate, not about what he wanted to do, but about procedures. He had to do the right thing. A captain goes last on to his ship, but a man goes first into a tricky situation. Nenna saw that the point had come, perhaps exactly as she tied up, when he was more at a loss than she was. Their sense of control wavered, ebbed, and changed places. She kicked off the wellingtons, which was easy enough, and began to go up the ladder.

'Is the hatch open?' she asked, thinking he would be more at ease if she said something entirely practical. On the other hand, it was a waste of words. The hatch on *Lord Jim* was always locked, but Richard never forgot the key.

9

NENNA's children neither showed any interest in where she had been nor in why she did not come back until next morning. Back again on *Grace*, Tilda was messing about at the foot of the mast with a black and yellow flag, one of the very few they had.

'We haven't much line either,' she said, 'I shall have to fly it from the stays.'

'What's it mean, Tilda dear?'

'This is L, *I have something important to communicate*. It was for you, Ma, in case you were out when we got back.'

'Where were you going, then?'

'We're going to take him out and show him round.'

'Who?'

'Heinrich.'

Martha came up the companion, followed by a boy very much taller than she was. Nenna was struck by the difference in her elder daughter since she had seen her last. Her hair was out of its fair pony tail and curled gracefully, with a life of its own, over her one and only Elvis shirt.

'Ma, this is Heinrich. He was sixteen three weeks ago. You don't know who he is.'

'I do know. Aunt Louise told me, but there was some kind of confusion in that she told me that he was due last Friday.'

'The date was altered, Mrs James,' Heinrich explained. 'I was delayed to some extent because the address given to me was 626 Cheyne Walk, which I could not find, but eventually the river police directed me.'

'Well, in any case I'd like to welcome you on board, Heinrich, hullo.'

'Mrs James. Heinrich von Furstenfeld.'

Heinrich was exceptionally elegant. An upbringing designed to carry him through changes of regime and frontier, possible loss of every worldly possession, and, in the event of crisis, protracted stays with distant relatives ensconced wherever the aristocracy was tolerated, from the Polish border to Hyde Park Gate, in short, a good European background, had made him totally self-contained and able with sunny smile and the formal handshake of the gymnast to set almost anybody at their ease, even the flustered Nenna.

'I hope Martha has shown you where to put your things.'

Martha looked at her impatiently.

'There's no need for him to unpack much, he's got to go to the airport tomorrow. He arrived here very late, and they had to find a bunk for him on *Rochester*. Willis was much more cheerful and said it reminded him of a boarding house in the old days.'

'I must go and explain to Mrs Woodie.'

'Oh, it's quite unnecessary. And I've shown Heinrich all round *Grace*. He understands that he can only go to the heads on a falling tide.'

'I am not so very used to calculating the tides, Mrs James,' said Heinrich in a pleasant conversational tone. 'The Danube, close to where I live, is not tidal, so that I shall have to rely for this information upon your charming daughters.'

'What's your house like in Vienna?' Tilda asked.

'Oh, it's a flat in the Franziskanerplatz, quite in the centre of things.'

'What kind of things are you used to doing in Vienna?' said Nenna. 'If you've only got one day in London, we shall have to see what we can arrange.'

'Oh, Vienna is an old city – I mean, everybody remarks on how many old people live there. So that although my native place is so beautiful, I am very much looking forward to seeing Swinging London.'

'Heinrich has to stand here on the deck while you drone on,' said Tilda. 'He ought to be given a cup of coffee immediately.'

'Oh, hasn't he had breakfast?'

'Ma, where are your shoes?' asked Martha, drawing her

mother aside and speaking in an urgent, almost tragic undertone. 'You look a mess. From Heinrich's point of view, you hardly look like a mother at all.'

'I don't know what his mother's like. I know his father's an old business acquaintance of Auntie Louise and Uncle Joel.'

'His mother is a Countess.'

Tilda had taken Heinrich below, and put a saucepan of milk on the gas for his coffee. To his dying day the young Count would not forget the fair hand which had tended him when none other had heeded his plight.

'Why is your mother barefoot?' Heinrich asked. 'But I won't press the query if it is embarrassing. Perhaps she is Swinging.'

'Oh, you'll get used to her.'

A diplomat by instinct, Heinrich considered which of his twenty or thirty smaller European cousins Tilda most resembled. The Swiss lot, probably. His tone became caressing and teasing.

'I shall have to take you back with me to Vienna, dear Tilda, yes, I'm sorry, I shan't be able to manage without you, fortunately you're so small they won't miss you here and I can take you for a Glücksbringer.'

Here he went astray, for Tilda did not at all like being so small. 'Get outside this,' she said, slamming the tin mug of coffee in front of him, and sawing away energetically at the loaf.

With a faint smile the young Count turned to thank

his saviour, while some colour stealed, stole, back into his pale cheeks.

On deck, Martha and Nenna had been joined by Maurice, who had decided to consider himself on holiday, and had not been to the pub for several nights.

'Who's the boy-friend?' he asked Martha.

'He is the son of the friend of my aunt.'

'Have it your own way. Pretty face, at all events.'

'Maurice,' said Martha. 'Help me. I'm trying to get my mother to dress and behave properly.'

It was just ten minutes to nine, and Richard walked by on his way up to World's End to catch a bus to the office. Nenna thought, if he doesn't look my way I'll never speak to him again, and in fact I'll never speak to any man again, except Maurice. But as he drew level with *Grace* Richard gave her a smile which melted her heart, and waved to her in a way entirely peculiar to himself, half way between a naval salute and a discreet gesture with the rolled umbrella.

Maurice folded his arms. 'Congratulations, Nenna.'

'Oh, don't say that.'

'Why not?'

'God made you too quick-witted. I don't know what's happening to me exactly.'

'Weak-mindedness.'

'Self-reproach, really.'

'What's that, dear?'

*   *   *

Martha left them, and went down the companion. Armed at all points against the possible disappointments of her life, conscious of the responsibilities of protecting her mother and sister, worried at the gaps in her education, anxious about nuns and antique dealers, she had forgotten for some time the necessity for personal happiness. Heinrich at first seemed strange to her.

The three children sat round the table and discussed how they were to spend the day. Tilda, unwatched by the other two, shook out the packets of cereal, at the bottom of which small plastic tanks, machine-guns and images of Elvis had been concealed by the manufacturers. When she had found the tokens she shovelled back the mingled wheat and rye, regardless, into the containers.

'You have no father, then, it seems, Martha,' Heinrich said quietly.

'He's left us.'

This was no surprise to Heinrich. 'My father, also, is often absent at our various estates.'

'You're archaic,' said Martha. Heinrich, while continuing to eat heartily, took her hand.

'I really came to bring you a telegram,' Maurice said. 'I fetched it from the boatyard office.'

'Did you, well, thank you, Maurice. I seemed to have missed some mail lately, my sister kept asking me whether I hadn't received her letters.'

'They have to take their chance with wind and tide, my dear, like all of us.'

The telegram was from Louise. They'd arrived in London. They were at the Carteret Hotel and Nenna was to call her there as soon as possible.

'Hullo, can I speak with Mrs Swanson? Hullo, is that Mr Swanson's room? Louise, it's Nenna.'

'Nenna, I was just about to ring you on that number I called before, from Frankfurt.'

'I'd as soon you didn't ring there, Louise.'

'Why, is there anything wrong?'

'Not exactly.'

'Is Edward with you, Nenna?'

'No.'

'That's what I anticipated. We want you to come and have lunch with us, dear.'

'Look, Louise, why don't I come over and see you both right away?'

'Lunch will be more convenient, dear, but after that we've put the whole of the rest of the day aside to have a thorough discussion of your problems. There seems to be so much to be settled. Joel is of one mind with me about this. I mean of course about yourself and the little girls, the possibility of your returning to Halifax.'

'It's the first time you've ever even mentioned this, Louise.'

'But I've been thinking about it, Nenna, and praying. Joel isn't a Catholic, as you know, but he's told me that he believes there's a Providence not so far away from us, really just above our heads if we could see it, that wants things to be the way they're eventually going. Now that idea appeals to me.'

'Listen, Louise, I went to see Edward yesterday.'

'I'm glad to hear it. Did he see reason?'

Nenna hesitated. 'I'm just as much to blame as he is and more. I can't leave him with nothing.'

'Where is he living?'

'With friends.'

'Well, he has friends, then.'

'Louise, you mustn't interfere.'

'Look, Nenna, we're not proposing anything so very sensational. I think we have to admit that you've tried and failed. And if we're offering you your passage home, you and the children, and help in finding your feet once you get there, and a good convent school for the girls, so that they can go straight on with the nuns and won't really notice any difference, well, all that's to be regarded as a loan, which we're very glad to offer you for an extended period, in the hopes of getting you back among caring people.'

'But there are people who care for me here too, Lou. I do wish you'd come and see *Grace*.'

'We must try and make time, dear. But you were always the one for boats — I'm always thankful to remember how happy that made father, the way you shared his feeling for boats and water. Tell me about your neighbours. Do you ever go and visit any of them?'

'We haven't any money,' said Martha, 'so you'll have to share our limited notion of entertainment.'

'There is nothing to be ashamed of in being poor,' said Heinrich.

'Yes, there is,' Martha replied, with a firmness which she could hardly have inherited either from her father or her mother, 'but there's no reason why we shouldn't go and look at things. Looking is seeing, really. That's what we do most of the time. We can go this afternoon and look at the King's Road.'

'I should like to visit a boutique,' said Heinrich.

'Well, that will be best about five or six, when everybody leaves work. A lot of them don't open till then.'

Tilda had lost interest in what was being said and had gone to fetch Stripey, who was being pursued across *Maurice* by a rat. Maurice was constantly being advised by Woodie and Richard to grease his mooring-ropes, so that the rats could not get across them, but he always forgot to do so.

Later in the day they prepared for their expedition into Chelsea. 'And your mother?' enquired Heinrich.

'You're always asking about her!' Martha cried. 'What do you think of her?'

'She is a very attractive woman for her years. But on the Continent we appreciate the woman of thirty.'

'Well, she's gone to talk things over with Aunt Louise, who's also an attractive woman for her years, but a good bit older, and quite different. She lives in Nova Scotia, and she's wealthy and energetic.'

'What do they talk over?'

'I expect Ma's arranging to take us out to Canada. She hasn't said so, but I should think it's that.'

'Then I shall see you often. We have relations both in Canada and in the United States.'

Martha tried not to wish, as they set out, that they could leave Tilda behind. She hardly remembered ever feeling this before about her ragged younger sister.

Without the guidance of the nuns, Tilda seemed to have lost her last vestige of moral sense. Partisan Street, the first street on the way up from the boats, was, as has been said, considered a rough place — a row of decrepit two-up, two-down brick houses, the refuge of crippled and deformed humanity. Whether they were poor because they were lame, or lame because they were poor, was perhaps a matter for sociologists, and a few years later, when their dwellings were swept away and replaced by council flats with rents much higher than they could afford, it must be assumed that they disappeared from the face of the earth. Tilda, who knew them all, loved to imitate them, and hobbled up Partisan

Street alternately limping and shuffling, with distorted features.

'Your sister makes me laugh, but I don't think it's right to do so,' Heinrich said.

Martha pointed out that everybody in the street was laughing as well. 'They've asked her to come and do it at their Christmas Club,' she said. 'I wish I could still laugh like that.'

They turned into World's End, and opened the door into the peaceful garden where the faithful of the Moravian sect lie buried.

'They're buried standing, so that on Judgement Day they can rise straight upward.'

'Men and women together?'

'No, they're buried separately.'

Shutting the door in the wall, they walked on, Martha conscious, through every nerve in her body, of Heinrich's hand under her elbow. She asked him what was the first sentence he had ever learned in English.

'I am the shoemaker's father.'

'And French?'

'I don't remember when I learned French. It must have been at some time, because I can speak it now. I can also get along on Polish and Italian. But I don't know that I shall ever make much use of these languages.'

'Everything that you learn is useful. Didn't you know

that everything you learn, and everything you suffer, will come in useful at some time in your life?'

'You got that from Mother Ignatius,' Tilda interrupted. 'Once, in the closing years of the last century, a poor woman earned her daily bread by working long hours at her treadle sewing machine. Work, work, ah it was all work I'm telling you in them days. Up and down, up and down, went that unwearying right foot of hers. And so by incessant exercise, her right foot grew larger and broader, while the other remained the same size, and at length she feared to go out in the streets at all, for fear of tripping and falling flat. Yet that woman, for all her tribulations, had faith in the intercessions of our Lady.'

'Tilda,' said Martha, stopping suddenly and taking her sister by the shoulders, 'I'll give you anything you like, within reason, to go back to the boats and stay there.'

Between the sisters there was love of a singularly pure kind, proof against many trials. Martha's look of request, or appeal, between her shadowing lashes, was one that Tilda would not disregard. Her protests were formal only.

'There's a lot more of that sewing-machine story.'

'I know there is.'

'I shall be all by myself. Ma's gone into London.'

'You must go to *Rochester*.'

'I've just been there.'

'Mrs Woodie told me she never finds the little ones a worry.'

'Perhaps she wishes she hadn't said that.'

'Willis will be there.'

Tilda alternately nodded her head and shook it violently from side to side. This meant consent.

'You must promise and vow to go straight to *Rochester*,' Martha told her. 'You must swear by the Sacred Heart. You know you like it there. You don't like it in the King's Road, because they won't let you into the boutiques, and you're too young to try on the dresses.'

Tilda darted off, hopping and skipping.

In this, its heyday, the King's Road fluttered, like a gypsy encampment, with hastily-dyed finery, while stage folk emerged from their beds at a given hour, to patrol the long pavements between Sloane Square and the Town Hall. Heinrich and Martha went in and out of one boutique after another, Dressing Down, Wearwithal, Wearabouts, Virtuous Heroin, Legs, Rags, Bags. A paradise for children, a riot of misrule, the queer looking shops reversed every fixed idea in the venerable history of commerce. Sellers, dressed in brilliant colours, outshone the purchasers, and, instead of welcoming them, either ignored them or were so rude that they could only have hoped to drive them away. The customers in return sneered at the clothing offered to them, and flung it on the ground. There were no prices, no sizes, no way to tell which stock was which, so that racks and rails of dresses were transferred as though by a magic hand from one shop to another. The doors stood open, breathing out incense and heavy soul, and the spirit was that of the market scene in the pantomine when the cast, encouraged by the audience, has let the business get out of hand.

Heinrich and Martha walked through this world, which was fated to last only a few years before the spell was broken, like a prince and princess. At Wearwithal, Heinrich tried on a pair of pale blue sateen trousers, which fitted tightly. Martha, guarding his jeans while he changed, admired him more for deciding against them than if he had bought them.

'Won't they do?' she asked.

'Such trousers are not worn on the Continent.'

'I thought perhaps you hadn't enough money.'

Heinrich in fact had plenty of money, and his own chequebook, but his delicacy, responding to Martha's pride, prevented him from saying so.

'We will go to a coffee bar.'

These, too, were something new in London, if not in Vienna. The shining Gaggia dispensed one-and-a-half inches of bitter froth into an earthenware cup, and for two shillings lovers could sit for many hours in the dark brown shadows, with a bowl of brown sugar between them.

'Perhaps they'll be annoyed if we don't have another cup.'

Heinrich again put his fine, long-fingered hand over

hers. She was amazed at its cleanliness. Her own hands were almost as black as Tilda's.

'You must not worry. I am in charge. How does that suit you?'

'I'm not sure. I'll tell you later,' said Martha, who wished one of her school friends would come in and see her. They'd tell Father Watson and the nuns, but what did that matter, they must know why she was absent from school anyway.

'I expect, living here in Chelsea, you go out a great deal.'

'How can I? I've no-one to go out with.'

'I think you would like the cake-shops in Vienna, also the concerts. I should like to present you to my mother and great-aunts. They take subscription tickets every winter for all the concerts, the *Musikverein*, anything you can name. You're fond of music?'

'Of course,' said Martha impatiently. 'What music do your great-aunts like?'

'Mahler. Bruckner . . .'

'I hate that. I don't want to be made to feel all the time.'

Heinrich put his head on one side and half closed his eyes.

'You know, I think that you could be heading for a very serious depression.' Martha felt flattered. It seemed to her that she had never been taken seriously before.

'You mean I could break down altogether?'

'Listen, Martha, the best thing would be for you to tell me about your worries. They are probably those with which your catechism class does not help. The nuns will not understand the physiological causes of your restlessness and priests do not know everything either. Perhaps you would rather I did not speak like this.'

'It's all right, Heinrich, go on.'

'I too, have many problems at school. About that you wouldn't understand very well, Martha. We are all of us youths between sixteen and eighteen years of age, and for month after month we are kept away from women. I, personally, have the number of days pasted up on the inside of my locker. All this can produce a kind of madness.'

'What do your teachers say?'

'The monks? Well, they comprehend, but they can't cover all our difficulties. A good friend of mine, in the same set for physics and chemistry, grew so disturbed that he took some scissors and cut all round the stiff white collars, which we have to wear on Sundays, and made them into little points.'

'Like a dog in a circus,' said Martha, appalled.

'He wanted to make himself grotesque. He has left school, but I received an air-letter from him recently. Now he is anxious to join the priesthood.'

'But are you happy there?'

Heinrich smiled at her consolingly. 'I shall not allow sex to dominate my life, I shall find a place for it, that is all . . . But, my dear, we are here to talk about you.'

She could see that he meant it, and knew that there might never again be such an opportunity.

'There's a great deal of sin in me,' she began rapidly. 'I know that a great part of me is darkness, not light. I wish my father and mother lived together, but not because I care whether they're happy or not. I love Ma, but she must expect to be unhappy because she's reached that time of life. I want them to live together in some ordinary kind of house so that I can come and say, how can you expect me to live here! But I shall never lead a normal life because I'm so short – we're both short – that's why Tilda stands on the deck half the day, it's because somebody told her that you only grow taller while you're standing up. And then I don't develop. We had a class composition, My Best Friend, and the girl who was describing me put up her hand and asked to borrow a ruler because she said she'd have to draw me straight up and down.'

'That is not friendship,' said Heinrich.

'There might be something wrong with me. I might be permanently immature.'

'I am sure you aren't, my dear. Listen, you are like the blonde mistress of Heine, the poet Heine, *wenig Fleisch, sehr viel Gemüt*, little body, but so much spirit'. He leaned forward and kissed her cheek, which, from being cold when they entered the coffee-bar, was now glowing pink. This was quite the right thing to do in a coffee-bar in the King's Road. But afterwards they became, for the time being, rather more distant.

'It has been very pleasant to spend the day here, Martha, and to see your boat.'

'Yes, well, at least that's something you haven't got in Vienna.'

Heinrich's father was a member of the Wiener Yacht Club.

'Certainly, not such a large one.'

Outside the boutiques were still aglow with heaps of motley flung about the feet of the disdainful assistants. The music grew louder, the Chelsea Granada welcomed all who would like to come in and watch the transmission of *Bootsie and Snudge*. They wandered on together at random.

'Two people can become close in a very short time,' Heinrich said. 'It is up to them not to let circumstances get the better of them. It is my intention, as I think I told you, to shape my own life.'

Tilda had not gone straight onto *Rochester*. Aware of the not quite familiar atmosphere which had surrounded Martha and Heinrich and detached her sister, she felt, for the first time, somewhat adrift. Jumping defiantly onto *Grace*'s deck, she gathered up the surprised Stripey and hugged her close. Then she examined her more attentively.

'You've got kittens on you.'

Depositing the cat, who flattened out immediately into a gross slumber, she swarmed up the mast. Low tide. A tug passed, flying a white house flag with the red cross of St George, and with a funnel that might have been either cream or white.

'Thames Conservancy. She oughtn't to be as far down-river as this. What's she doing below Teddington?'

On *Maurice*, fifteen feet below her, Harry, in the owner's absence, was unusually busy. He was wiring up the main hatch above the hold, in such a way that showed he was certainly not an electrician by trade, with the intention of giving a mild electric shock to anyone who might try to get into it.

Tilda did not understand what he was doing, but she stared at him from the height of the mast until he became conscious of her, and turned round. He put down his pliers and looked up at her. His eyes were curious, showing an unusual amount of the whites.

'Want some sweeties?'

'No.'

'Want me to show you a comic?'

'No.'

'Come on, you can't read, can you?'

'I can.'

'You could get over here, couldn't you? You can come and sit on my knee if you like and I'll show you a comic.'

Tilda swung to and fro, supported by only one arm round the mast.

'Have you got *Cliff Richard Weekly*?'

'Oh, yes, I've got that.'

'And *Dandy*?'

'Yes, I've got that too.'

'This week's?'

'That's right.'

'I don't need showing.'

'You haven't seen the things I've got to show you.'

'What are they like?'

'Something you've never seen before, love.'

'You've no right on that boat,' Tilda remarked. 'She belongs to Maurice.'

'Know him, then?'

'Of course I do.'

'Know what he does for a living?'

'He goes out to work.'

'I'll show you what he does, if you like. You won't find that in a comic.'

Tilda persisted. 'Why are you putting up wires on *Maurice*?'

'Why? Well, I've got a lot of nice things in here.'

'Where did you get them from?'

'Don't you want to know what they are?'

'No, I want to know where you got them from.'

'Why?'

'Because you're a criminal.'

'Who told you that, you nasty little bitch?'

'You're a receiver of stolen goods,' Tilda replied.

She watched him sideways, her eyes alight and alive.
After all, there were only two ways that Harry could come
on to *Grace*, the gangplank across from *Maurice*, on which
Stripey lay digesting uneasily, or back to the wharf and
round by the afterdeck.

Harry bent down and with one hand lifted the gangplank so that it hung in mid-air. Stripey shot upwards,
sprang, and missed her footing, falling spreadeagled on
the foreshore.

'Your kitty's split open, my love.'

'No, she's not. She's been eating a seagull. If she was
open you'd see all the feathers.'

Harry had a bottle in his hand.

'Are you going to get drunk?'

'The stuff in this bottle? Couldn't drink that. It would
burn me if I did. It'd fucking well burn anybody.'

It was spirits of salt. He looked at her with the points
of his eyes, the whites still rolling. The bottle was in his
right hand and he swung it to and fro once or twice,
apparently judging its weight. Then he moved towards
the wharf, coming round to meet her on *Grace*.

Tilda clambered over the washboard, and clinging on by fingers and toes to the strakes, half slithered and half climbed down the side, gathered up the cat and skimmed across to *Rochester*. The side-ladder was out, as she very well knew.

'Oh, Mrs Woodie, will you look after me? Martha told me to come here. I came here straight away.'

'What's that you're carrying?' asked Mrs Woodie, resigned by now to almost anything.

'She's my pet, my pet, the only pet I've been allowed to have since I was a tiny kiddie.'

Mrs Woodie looked at the distended animal.

'Are you sure, dear, that she's not . . .'

'What do you mean, Mrs Woodie? I believe that there's an angel that guards her footsteps.'

The hold of *Rochester* had changed, in the last few weeks, from below decks to a cosy caravan interior. There was a good piece of reversible carpet put down, and Tilda seated herself, open-mouthed, in front of the television, where *Dr Kildare* flickered. Mrs Woodie began to cut sandwiches into neat squares. 'Where are you?' she called to her husband.

Woodie appeared, somewhat put out. 'I'll take a cup to Willis. He's still dwelling too much on the past, in my opinion.'

'Tell him Tilda's here.'

Willis came in quietly and sat beside the child on the

locker, covered with brand new flower-patterned cushions.

'Where's your sister?'

'Out with Heinrich.'

'With the German lad? Well, he seems nice enough. He wouldn't remember the war, of course.'

Tilda began to tell him exactly what had been happening in *Dr Kildare*, so far. She said nothing about Harry, because, for the time being, she had forgotten all about him.

Richard came back from work that evening later than he had hoped. Disappointed that there were no lights showing on *Grace* – it had never occurred to him that Nenna would not be there tonight – he was turning to walk along the Embankment to *Lord Jim* when he caught sight of a stranger on *Maurice*. He therefore changed direction and went along the wharf.

'I'm a friend of the owner's,' he said. 'Good evening.'

There was no reply, and he noticed that the gangplank was down between *Maurice* and *Grace*. Something was not quite right, so without hesitation he dropped down onto the deck.

Harry did not look up, but continued paying out the flex until he rounded the corner of the deck-house and could see Richard without bothering to turn his head. He put down the pair of pliers he was holding and picked up a heavy adjustable spanner.

'What are you doing on this boat?' Richard asked.

'Who made you God here?' said Harry.

The light was fading to a point where the battlements of the Hovis tower could only just be distinguished from the pinkish-grey of the sky. When Richard came a couple of steps nearer — it would never have occurred to him to go back until the matter was satisfactorily settled — Harry, looking faintly surprised, as though he couldn't believe that anything could be quite so simple, raised the adjustable spanner and hit him on the left side of the head, just below the ear. Richard fell without much sound. He folded up sideways against the winch, and immediately tried to get up again. It would have been better if he had been less conscientious, because he had broken one of his ribs against the handle of the winch and as he struggled to his feet the sharp broken edge of the bone penetrated slightly into his lung. Harry watched him fall back and noted that a considerable quantity of blood was coming away at the mouth. He wiped the spanner and put it away with his other tools. He was reflecting, perhaps, that this had been an easier job than the electrical wiring. Carrying the bag of tools, he disappeared up the wharf towards Partisan Street and the King's Road.

Heinrich and Martha were walking back to the Reach hand in hand. 'That's Maurice's pub,' she told him, 'he'll be in there now,' and, as they got nearer, 'I wish the Venice lantern was still there, it looked nice at night,' but in reality there was no need to say very much.

The foreshore was dark as pitch, but the corner street lamps palely illuminated the deck of *Maurice*. The body of a man lay across the winch, with an arm drooped over the side.

'Martha, don't look.'

Often, as the night drew on, a number of people were seen to lie down in odd places, both in Partisan Street and on the Embankment. Maurice's customers, too, were unpredictable. But none of them lay still in quite this way.

'Perhaps it's Harry,' Martha said. 'If it is, and he's dead, it'll be a great relief for Maurice.'

They walked steadily nearer, and saw blood on the deck, looking blackish in the dim light.

'It's *Lord Jim*,' she whispered.

The sight of a lord, knocked out by criminals, exactly fitted in with Heinrich's idea of Swinging London.

'It's Mr Blake,' said Martha.

'What should we do?'

Martha knew that with any luck the police launch would be at *Bluebird*. 'They go there to fetch the nurses on night shift and give them a lift down to hospital.'

'That would not be permitted in Vienna.'

'It's not permitted here.'

They were both running along the Embankment.

Loud music, complained of by the neighbours on shore, thumped and echoed from cheerful *Bluebird* on the middle Reach. You could have told it a mile away. The river police duty-boat, smart as a whistle, was waiting alongside.

In this way Richard, still half-alive, was admitted to the men's casualty ward of the Waterloo Hospital. One of the young probationers from *Bluebird* was on the ward, and came in with an injection for him, to help him to go to sleep.

'Isn't it Miss Jackson?' Richard said faintly. He had been trained to recognise anybody who had served under him, or who had helped him in any way. Miss Jackson had assisted with the removal of Willis. But Richard's polite attempt to straighten himself and to give something like a slight bow made the damage to his lung rather worse.

They patched him up, and he dozed through the night.

The long pallid hospital morning passed with interruptions from the nursing, cleaning, and auxiliary staff, all of whom gravitated to the bed, where they were received by the nice-looking Mr Blake, who was in terrible pain, with grave correctness. The probationers told him to remember that every minute he was getting a little better, and Ward Sister told him not to make any effort, and not to try to take anything by the mouth. 'I'm afraid I'm being a bit of a nuisance,' Richard tried to say. 'You're not supposed to talk,' they said.

When he was left to himself his mind cleared, and he began to reflect. He remembered falling, and the deck coming up to hit him, which brought back the sensation – although it hadn't done so at the time – of the moment just before the torpedo hit *Lanark*. He also remembered the look of the adjustable spanner, and it seemed to him appropriate that having been knocked down with a spanner his whole body was now apparently being alternately wrenched and tightened. There must surely be some connection of ideas here, and he would get better quickly if he could be certain that everything made sense.

Next, having reviewed, as well as he could, his work at the office, and made a courageous but unsuccessful attempt to remember whether there was any urgent correspondence he hadn't dealt with, he let his thoughts return to Nenna. Yesterday, or was it the day before yesterday, or when was it, he had gone first up the ladder on to *Lord Jim*, but Nenna had gone first into the cabin. Thinking about this, he felt happier, and then quite at peace. It was rather a coincidence that she was wearing a dark blue guernsey exactly like Laura's, with a neck which necessitated the same blindfold struggle to get it off. About the whole incident Richard felt no dissatisfaction and certainly no regret. He could truly reflect that he had done not only the best, but the only thing possible.

At the end of the morning a very young doctor made his rounds and told Richard on no account to talk, he was only making a routine check-up. 'You can answer with simple signs,' he said reassuringly, 'we'll soon have you out of here and on four wheels again.' Less sensitive than the nurses, he evidently took Richard for a quarrelsome garage proprietor.

'No bleeding from the ears?'

The young houseman appeared to be consulting a list, and Richard, anxious to help a beginner, tried to indicate that he would bleed from the ears if it was the right thing to do. As to the exact locality of the pain, it was difficult to convey that it had grown, and that instead of having a pain he was now contained inside it. The doctor told him that they would be able to give him something for that.

'And absolute quiet, no police as yet. We had an officer here wanting you to make a statement, but he'll have to wait a couple of days. However,' he added unexpectedly, 'we're going to bend the regulations a little bit and let you see your children.'

From the no-man's land at the entrance to the ward, where the brown lino changed to blue, Tilda's voice could be heard, asking whether she and her sister might be allowed to bring Mr Blake a bottle of Suncrush.

'Is he your Daddy, dear?'

'He is, but we haven't seen him for many, many years, for more than we can remember.'

'Well, if Dr Sawyer's given permission . . .'

Tilda advanced, with Martha lingering doubtfully behind, and swept several plants from the loaded windowsill to make room for the Suncrush.

'Do you remember us, Daddy dear?'

Ward Sister was still complaining that children were not allowed to see the patients unattended. By good fortune, however, another visitor arrived; it was Willis, who took charge at once of the two girls. Richard's catastrophe had brought him to himself. Gratitude, felt by most people as a burden, was welcome to the unassuming Willis.

'Well, Skipper, it's sad to see you laid low. Not so long since I was in here myself, but I never dreamed . . .'

Willis had not quite known what to bring, so he'd decided on a packet of Whiffs. In his ward at the Waterloo they'd been allowed to smoke for an hour a day. 'But I can see it's different in here,' he said, as though this, too, was a mark of the superiority of Skipper. Richard did not smoke, but Willis had never noticed this.

'I think he wants to write something for you, dear,' the nurse said to Martha. Tilda, unabashed, was out in the pantry, helping the ward orderlies take the lids off the supper trays. Richard looked at Martha and saw Nenna's puzzled eyes, though they were so much darker. He painfully scrawled on the piece of paper which had been left for him: HOW IS YOUR MOTHER?

Martha wrote in turn – it didn't occur to her to say

it aloud, although Richard could hear perfectly well —
BUSY, SHE'S PACKING.

WHAT FOR?

WE'RE GOING TO CANADA.

WHEN?

But this Martha could not answer.

Laura was sent for, and arrived back in London the
following afternoon. She dealt easily and efficiently with
Richard's office, with the police, with the hospital. There
she spoke only to Matron and the lung specialist. 'It's
no use talking to the ward staff, they're so overworked,
poor dears, they can't tell one case from another!' The
ward sister had actually drawn her aside and asked her
whether she did not think it would be a good idea to let
her husband see his children more often in the future.

Richard was still not allowed to speak — he was not
recovering quite so fast as had been expected — and he
could make little reply when Laura told him that this was
exactly the kind of thing she had expected all along, and
that she would see about disposing of *Lord Jim* immediately.
Her family, applied to, began to scour the countryside for
a suitable house, within reasonable commuting distance
from London, in good condition, and recently decorated,
so that she could move Richard straight there as soon as
he was discharged from hospital.

10

NENNA felt that she could have made a better hand at answering Louise if only Edward had taken the trouble to return her purse. It wasn't only the money, but her library card, her family allowance book, the receipt from the repair shop without which she couldn't get her watch back, creased photographs, with Edward's own photograph among them, her address book, almost the whole sum of her identity.

After all, she thought, if she did go away, how much difference would it make? In a sense, Halifax was no further away than 42b Milvain Street, Stoke Newington. All distances are the same to those who don't meet.

Halifax was equally far from the Norfolk border, to which Laura had removed Richard. The FOR SALE notice nailed to *Lord Jim*'s funnel saddened her and if possible she approached *Grace* from the other direction. If she had told Richard about Harry, and about *Maurice*'s dubious cargo, he wouldn't have had to lie in a pool of blood waiting for her own daughter to rescue him. But curiously enough the regret she felt, not for anything she had done but for what she hadn't, quite put an end to the old wearisome illusion of prosecution and trial. She no longer felt that she needed to defend herself, or even to account for herself, there. She was no longer of any interest to Edward. The case was suspended indefinitely.

As Louise seemed unwilling to come to the boats, Nenna was obliged to take the girls to tea at the luxurious Carteret. It was an anxious business to make them sufficiently respectable. On the twelfth floor of the hotel, from which they could just get a view of the distant river, they were delighted with their prosperous-looking aunt. Taller, stronger, not so blonde but much more decisive than their mother, she still seemed perpetually astonished by life.

'Martha! Tilda! Well I'll be! I haven't seen you both for such a long time, and you're both of you just! Well, how are you going to like us in Canada?'

'Louise, that depends on such a number of things. We have to sell *Grace*, to begin with.'

'What would happen if I pressed that bell?' Tilda asked.

'Well, somebody would come along, one of the floor waiters, to ask if we wanted tea, or cakes, or any little thing like that. Go on, you can press it, honey.'

Tilda did so. The bell was answered, and their order arrived.

'Is that right, dear?'

'Yes, those are the things Martha and I like. Are there any boats in Canada?'

'No shortage of boats, no shortage of water.'

Tilda's mind was made up in favour of the New World.

'But I'm not sure that we ought to leave Maurice, though,' she said, licking each finger in turn. 'Now that he won't have Ma to talk to, and there's no Mr Blake to get up a subscription if he goes down, I'd say he might lose heart altogether. And then the police are always coming round to interrogate him.'

'Who's Maurice, dear?' asked her aunt rather sharply.

'Maurice is on *Maurice*, just like the Blakes were on *Lord Jim*.'

'Ah, yes, Richard Blake, he called me up.'

'How could he?' Nenna cried.

'You remember, he's the one I had to call his number to get you, that's when we were in Frankfurt. I told him then that when we came to England we'd be staying at this hotel. It suits us all right, although Joel keeps saying that the service was so much better before the war.'

'But what did he say?'

Nenna's question caused confusion, which Louise gradually sorted out. What had this Richard Blake said, well, she got the impression that he was counting on coming to a series of Transatlantic insurance conferences in the spring, and he was either coming to Montreal first, or to New York, she couldn't remember which order it was, search me, said Louise, she hadn't thought it mattered all that much.

'I don't know whether it does or not,' said Nenna. 'He was going to show me how to fold up a map properly.'

'Joel can do that for you, dear.'

'We shan't be able to take Stripey,' said Tilda, continuing the course of her own thoughts. 'She won't leave *Grace*. Mrs Woodie bought her a basket, a very nice one made by the blind, but she wouldn't get into it.'

'Mrs Woodie?'

'A kindly lady, somewhat advanced in years.'

'She'll enjoy being back at school with girls of her own age,' Louise quietly observed to Nenna.

Mr Swanson came in, greeted everybody, and ordered a rye.

'Well, von Furstenfeld called me today, their boy's arrived safely in Vienna, and they're more than pleased, Nenna, with the spirit of hospitality you and your family extended to him. I owe you a debt of gratitude there.'

Martha smiled, perfectly tranquil.

Joel Swanson did not understand, nor did he ever expect to understand, exactly what was going on, but the kind of activity he seemed to be hearing about, in snatches only, was more or less exactly what he'd expect from his wife's relatives. He smiled at them with inclusive good will.

★ ★ ★

With *Lord Jim* and *Grace* both on his books, Pinkie felt doubtful about his chance of selling either. Of course, they were at the opposite ends of the price range. But the market would be affected, particularly as the disappointed broker hadn't hesitated to tell everyone how lucky he'd been not to drop a packet on *Dreadnought*, which had gone straight to the bottom like a stone in a pond. It was awkward, too, from the sales point of view, that Richard had been aboard one of these barges when he got knocked over the head. Thank heavens he hadn't got to try and sell that one. Poor old Richard, torpedoed three times, and then finished off, near as a toucher, with an adjustable spanner. Pinkie consulted the senior partner.

'Not everyone's buy. But if someone's looking for an unusual night spot . . .'

On *Grace* there was, after all, not so very much to be done. The barges, designed to be sailed by one man and a boy, could be laid up in a few days. Only the mast gave trouble. Not all Woodie's efforts could succeed in lowering it. 'I've another idea about your mast,' he said every morning, coming brightly across, but the thick rust held it fast. As to the packing, Mrs Woodie, eager to give a hand, was disappointed to find so little to do. The James family seemed to have few possessions. Mrs Woodie felt half inclined to lend her some, so as to have more to sort out and put away.

Unperturbed, Stripey gave birth. The warm hold of

Rochester was chosen by the sagacious brute, and Willis, always up very early, found her on the ruins of the new locker cushions, with five mud-coloured kittens. Martha presented all but one to Father Watson. The presbytery needed a cheerful touch, he had so often hinted at this. But the priest, who had a strong instinct of self-preservation, transferred the litter of river-animals to the convent, as prizes in the Christmas raffle. With relief, he discussed the emigration of the James family with the nuns; so much the best thing – if there was no chance of a reconciliation – all round.

The night before Nenna and her two daughters were due to leave England, storm weather began to blow up on the Reach. There had been a good deal of rain, the Thames was high, and a north-westerly had piled up water at the river's mouth, waiting for a strong flood tide to carry it up. Before dark the wind grew very strong.

A storm always seems a strange thing in a great city, where there are so many immoveables. In front of the tall rigid buildings the flying riff-raff of leaves and paper seemed ominous, as though they were escaping in good time. Presently, larger things were driven along, cardboard boxes, branches, and tiles. Bicycles, left propped up, fell flat. You could hear glass smashing, and now pieces of broken glass were added to the missiles which the wind flung along the scoured pavement. The Embankment, swept clean, was deserted. People came out of the Underground and, leaning at odd angles to meet the wind, hurried home from work by the inner streets.

Above the river, the seagulls kept on the wing as long as they could, hoping the turbulence would bring them a good find, then, defeated and battered, they heeled and screamed away to find refuge. The rats on the wharf behaved strangely, creeping to the edge of the planking, and trying to cross over from dry land to the boats.

On the Reach itself, there could be no pretence that this would be an ordinary night. Tug skippers, who had never before acknowledged the presence of the moored barges, called out, or gave the danger signal – five rapid blasts in succession. Before slack tide the police launch went down the river, stopping at every boat to give fair warning.

'Excuse me, sir, have you checked your anchor recently?'

The barge anchors were unrecognisable as such, more like crustaceans, specimens of some giant type long since discarded by Nature, but still clinging to their old habitat, sunk in the deep pits they had made in the foreshore. But under the ground they were half rusted away. *Dreadnought*'s anchor had come up easily enough when the salvage tug came to dispose of her. The mud which held so tenaciously could also give way in a moment, if conditions altered.

'And how much anchor chain have you got? The regulation fifteen fathoms? All in good condition?'

Like many questions which the police were obliged to put, these were a formality, it being clear that the barge-owners couldn't answer them. It could only be hoped that the mooring-ropes were in better case than the anchors. The visit was, in fact, a courteous excuse to leave a note of the nearest Thames Division telephone number.

'Waterloo Pier. WAT 5411. In all emergencies. Sure you've got that?'

'We'd have to go on shore to telephone,' said Woodie doubtfully, when his turn came. He was thinking of taking *Rochester*'s complement straight to Purley in the car, whether Willis agreed or not.

'What do you think of this weather, officer?'

The sergeant understood him, as one Englishman to another. The wind had ripped the tarpaulin off some of the laid-up boats, and huge fragments of oilcloth were flying at random, wrapping themselves round masts and rails.

'You want to look out for those,' he said. 'They could turn nasty.'

The Thames barges, built of living wood that gave and sprang back in the face of the wind, were as much at home as anything on the river. To their creaking and grumbling was added a new note, comparable to music.

As the tide rose, the wind shredded the clouds above them and pushed a mighty swell across the water, so that they began to roll as they had once rolled at sea.

Nenna and Martha had absolutely forbidden Tilda to go above decks. Banished to the cabin, she lay there full of joy, feeling the crazy desire of the old boat to put out once again into mid-stream. Every time *Grace* rose on the swell, she was aware of the anchor chain tightening to its limit.

'We're all going ashore,' Nenna called, '*Rochester*'s gone already. We're just taking a bag, we'll come back for the rest when the wind's gone down.'

Tilda put on her anorak. She thought them all cowards.

No-one knew that Maurice was on board ship, because there were no lights showing. Certainly not a habitual drinker, he was nevertheless sitting that night in the darkness with a bottle of whisky, prepared for excess.

It wasn't the uncertain nature of his livelihood that worried him, nor the police visits, although he had twice been invited to accompany the officers to the station. So far they hadn't applied for a search warrant to go over the boat, but Maurice didn't care if they did. Still less did he fear the storm. The dangerous and the ridiculous were necessary to his life, otherwise tenderness would overwhelm him. It threatened him now, for what

Maurice had not been able to endure was the sight of the emptying Reach. *Dreadnought, Lord Jim*, now *Grace*. Maurice, in the way of business, knew too many, rather than too few, people, but when he imagined living without friends, he sat down with the whisky in the dark.

When he heard steps overhead on deck, he switched on the light. Making two shots at it before he could manage the switch, he wondered if he'd better not drink any more. Of course, that rather depended on who was coming; he didn't know the footsteps. Someone was blundering about, didn't know the boat, probably didn't know about boats at all, couldn't find the hatch. Maurice, always hospitable, went to open it. His own steps seemed enormous, he floated up the steps, swimming couldn't be so difficult after all, particularly as he'd become weightless. Reaching the hatch at the same time as the stranger outside, he collided with it, and they fell into each other's arms. Not a tall man, quite young and thin, and just as drunk, to Maurice's relief, as he was.

'My name's James.'

'Come in.'

'This is a boat, isn't it?'

'Yes.'

'Is it *Grace*?'

'No.'

'Pity.'

'You said your name was James?'

'No, Edward.'

'Never mind.'

Edward took a bottle of whisky out of his pocket and, unexpectedly, two glasses. The glasses made Maurice sad. They must have been brought in the hope of some celebration to which the way had been lost.

'Clever of you to come on the right night,' he said.

He was absorbed, as host, in the task of getting his guest safely below decks. Fortunately he had had a good deal of practice in this. As he filled the glasses his depression emptied away.

Edward, sitting down heavily on the locker, said that he wanted to explain.

'Doctors tell you not to drink too much. They're very insistent on this. They're supported by teams of physiologists and laboratory researchers.'

He steered his way round these words much as he had negotiated the deck.

'What these so-called scientists should be doing is to study effects. Take my case. If one whisky makes me feel cheerful, four whiskies ought to make me feel very cheerful. Agreed?'

'I'm with you.'

'They haven't. I've had four whiskies and I feel wretched. Bloody wretched. Take that from me. And now I'd like to leave you with this thought . . .'

'Do you have to make many speeches in the course of your work?' Maurice asked.

For an instant Edward sobered up. 'No, I'm clerical.'

The barge took a great roll, and Maurice could hear the hanger with his good suit in it, waiting for the job which never came, sliding from one end of its rail to the other.

'I came to give Nenna a present,' Edward said. Out of the same pocket which had held the glasses he produced a small blue and gold box.

'There's a bottle of scent in this box.'

'What kind?'

'It's called L'Heure Bleue.'

'Do you mind if I write that down?' Maurice asked.

'Certainly. Have my biro.'

'It's the Russian for "pen", you know.'

'Hungarian.'

'Russian.'

'A Hungarian invented them.'

'He would have made a fortune if.'

'What's so special about this scent? You brought it for Nenna. Does she wear it?'

'I don't know. I think perhaps not. I haven't much sense of smell.'

'I don't think Nenna uses scent at all.'

'Do you know her, then?'

They both emptied their glasses.

'The mother whose man I live of the house in suggested it,' said Edward.

'What?'

'Wasn't that clear? I'm afraid I'm losing my fine edge.'

'Not a bit of it.'

'Gordon said I ought to bring her some scent.'

From directly above them came a noise like an explosion in a slate quarry. Something heavy had been torn away and, bouncing twice, landed flat on the deck directly over their heads. The deck timbers screamed in protest. Edward seemed to notice nothing.

'I've brought her purse.'

This too he dragged and tugged out of his pocket, and they both stared at it as though by doing so they could turn it into something else.

'Do you think she'll take me back?'

'I don't know,' Maurice said doubtfully. 'Nenna loves everybody. So do I.'

'Oh, do you know Nenna, then?'

'Yes.'

'You must know her pretty well, living on the same boat.'

'The next boat.'

'I expect she sometimes comes to borrow sugar. Matches, she might borrow.'

'We're both borrowers.'

'She's not easy to understand. You could spend a very long time, trying to understand that woman.'

There was about a quarter of the bottle left, and Edward poured it out for both of them. This time the movement of the boat helped him, and *Maurice* rocked the whisky out in two curves, one for each glass.

'Do you understand women?'

'Yes,' said Maurice.

With a great effort, holding his concentration as though he had it in his two hands, he added,

'You've got to give these things to her. Give them, that's it, give them. You've got to go across to *Grace*.'

'How's that done?'

'It's not difficult. Difficult if you're heavy. Luckily we haven't any weight this evening.'

'How do I go?'

It was worse than ever getting up the companion, much worse than last time. The whole boat plunged, but not now in rhythm with the staggering of Maurice and Edward. They managed three steps. The hatch in front of them flew open and the frame, tilted from one side to the other, gave them a sight of the wild sky outside. A rat was sitting at the top of the companion. A gleam of light showed its crossed front teeth. Edward struggled forward.

'Brute, I'll get it.'

'It's one of God's creatures!' cried Maurice.

Edward hurled all that he had in his hands, the purse, the scent, which struck the rat in the paunch. Hissing loudly, it swivelled on its hind legs and disappeared, the tail banging like a rope on the top step as it fled.

'Did the scent break?'

'I can smell it, I'm afraid.'

'I came here to give her a present.'

'I know, James.'

'What do I give her now?'

Edward sat empty-handed on the companion. Maurice, who still hadn't exactly made out who he was, suddenly cared intensely about the loss.

'Another present.'

'What?'

'Hundreds. I've got hundreds.'

Clinging together they followed the line of the keelson to the forward hatch.

'Hundreds!'

Record-players, electric guitars, transistors, electric hair-curlers, electric toasters, Harry's hoard, the strange currency of the 1960s, piled on the floor, on the bunks, all in their new containers, all wrapped in plastic. Maurice snatched out a pile and loaded them on to the reeling Edward.

'She'll find these useful on *Grace*.'

'How do I get there?'

* * *

How had they got back on deck? As the battering wind seized them they had to stoop along in the darkness, fighting for handholds, first the base of the old pulley, then the mast. Three toasters sailed away like spindrift in the gale. It was still blowing hard north-west. The gang-plank to *Grace* was missing. The crash above their heads had come when it was lifted bodily and flung across the deck.

'There's still the ladder.'

Maurice had a fixed iron ladder down the port side.

'Is that *Grace*?' Edward shouted above the wind.

'Yes.'

'Can't see any lights.'

'Of course you can't. It's dark.'

'I hadn't thought of that. Don't know much about boats.'

Edward was much more confused than Maurice and needed all the help he was getting as Maurice manhandled him to the top of the ladder. Maurice was still sober enough to know that he was drunk, and knew also that the water between the boats was wilder than he had ever seen it. That something was dreadfully wrong was an idea which urgently called his attention, but it wavered beyond his grasp. It was to do with getting over to *Grace*.

'This isn't the usual way we go.'

Edward had dropped the whole cargo of gifts by the time he had got down the twenty iron rungs of the ladder.

As he reached the bottom the whole boat suddenly heaved away from him, so that the washboard at the top rolled out of sight and a quite new reach of sky appeared.

'Look out!'

Maurice was half-collapsed over the gunwale. Even like that, hopelessly drunk and quite tired out, there was about him an appealing look of promise, of everything that can be meant by friendship.

'You must come again when the weather's better!'

He leaned out, perilously askew, just to catch a sight of Edward's white face at the bottom of the ladder. Edward shouted back something that the wind carried away, but he seemed to be saying, once again, that he was not very used to boats.

With that last heave, Maurice's anchor had wrenched clear of the mud, and the mooring-ropes, unable to take the whole weight of the barge, pulled free and parted from the shore. It was in this way that *Maurice*, with the two of them clinging on for dear life, put out on the tide.

PENELOPE FITZGERALD

The Beginning of Spring

SHORTLISTED FOR THE BOOKER PRIZE

Frank Reid is a struggling Moscow printer of English extraction. On the eve of the First World War his wife Nellie inexplicably flies home to Blighty, leaving him to raise their three young children alone. How does Frank cope? Should he listen to the advice of his bookkeeper, Selwyn Crane, a poet and devotee of Tolstoy? And should he, in his wife's absence, resist his desire for his lovely, if mysterious, Russian housemaid? *The Beginning of Spring* is a virtuoso evocation of a time and a place, scrupulously written, subtle and endlessly surprising.

'This is a marvellous, intelligent and beautifully crafted book'   *Daily Telegraph*

PENELOPE FITZGERALD

The Gate of Angels

SHORTLISTED FOR THE BOOKER PRIZE

Cambridge University, 1912. Fred Fairly, a junior fellow at the all-male College of St Angelicus, believes that religion and the mysteries of the universe will soon be routed by rational science. After a freakish cycling accident, however, he encounters the shapely form of Daisy Saunders, a bright, forthright young nurse, who forces him to reassess his attitude to the whole mind-body problem. A love story ablaze with ideas, *The Gate of Angels* was shortlisted for the Booker Prize in 1990.

'An exquisite *tour de force*'   *Independent on Sunday*

THE SUNDAY TIMES

WIN £1000 OF
waterstone's VOUCHERS!

To celebrate The Sunday Times Contemporary Collection at Waterstone's, we are offering you the chance to win £1000 to spend at Waterstone's.

To enter, either go online to **thesundaytimes.co.uk/collection** or fill in the form below and send it to: Waterstone's 99p Books, Times House, 1 Pennington Street, London E98 1TT

Title Mr ☐ Mrs ☐ Miss ☐ Ms ☐ Other ☐

Name ....

Address ....

Postcode...DoB ....

Day tel...

Mobile*...

Email*..

In a typical week, how often do you buy The Times?

4-6 times ☐ 1-3 times ☐
Less than once a week ☐ Never ☐

In a typical month, how often do you buy The Sunday Times?

1-2 times per month ☐ 3-4 times per month ☐
Less than once a month ☐ Never ☐

*By supplying your mobile number and email address you are happy to receive offers via email/SMS from or in association with Times Newspapers Limited. Times Newspapers Limited directly (or via its agents) may mail or phone you about new promotions, products and services. Tick if you don't want to receive these from us or carefully selected companies (see our privacy policy at nidp.com). ☐

Terms and conditions: You must be over 18 years old to enter. Competition closes at midnight on August 14, 2011. Winners will be selected at random from the correct entries.